One Girl, Two Decks, Three Degrees of L♥ve

Jonny Zucker lives with his wife and two young children in North London. He always wanted to be an author and he wrote loads of stories while at school. However, he was always being told off for: a) writing stories when he should be listening, and b) plotting the downfall of the teachers.

After university Jonny realised he needed to get a 'proper job' so that he could afford to buy basic items – like food – so he trained and worked as a teacher. He spent much of his time in school: a) writing stories when he should be in class, and b) keeping his eye out for pupils plotting the downfall of the teachers. He supplemented his teaching income by writing part-time, composing songs for a children's theatre company and doing stand-up comedy gigs in the evenings.

Eventually he started to write full-time and has now written over thirty books for children, teenagers and adults. *One Girl, Two Decks, Three Degrees of Love* is his first book for Piccadilly Press.

One Girl, Two Decks, Three Degrees of Love

JONNY ZUCKER

PICCADILLY PRESS • LONDON

For Fiona

First published in Great Britain in 2004
by Piccadilly Press Ltd,
5 Castle Road, London NW1 8PR
www.piccadillypress.co.uk

A catalogue record for this book is available from the British Library

ISBN: 1 85340 810 7 (trade paperback)

1 3 5 7 9 10 8 6 4 2

Printed and bound in Great Britain by Bookmarque Ltd
Cover design by Louise Millar
Text design by Judith Robertson
Set in GillSans Light

'How many times do I have to tell you, Zoe? Turn it down!'

I looked up from the twin record decks at my mum, standing in the bedroom doorway and shooting her spikiest glare at me.

I was monitoring the track I was lining up through one headphone covering my left ear. The other headphone was resting behind my right ear, so I could listen to the track coming out of the speakers.

'You're fourteen, Zoe, you know the score,' she snarled. 'Some of us are trying to earn money, so that people like you can be fed and clothed.'

Here we go again — the old guilt trip routine. It's one of her favourites. I reckon she spends hours in front of the mirror perfecting it to achieve maximum impact.

It was a Tuesday — one of those bright September late afternoons. I'd only been back at school a few weeks, and thankfully the teachers hadn't started persecuting us yet. I was hoping to get a long mixing session in before supper. Mum clearly didn't share my enthusiasm for this idea.

Reaching for the up fader, I killed the speakers. This generous act would have satisfied most people on the planet, but not Mum. She didn't show the slightest indication of budging. The tune continued to spill out from the headphones, which were now nestling around my neck.

'I can still hear it,' she said crossly.

I sighed as loudly as I could, removed the headphones and put them down on my mixer. I carefully lifted the needles off both records and my room was suddenly silent.

'Happy now?' I enquired sulkily.

'There's a crucial deadline tomorrow,' she informed me. 'And not surprisingly, I'm finding it hard to concentrate. It's a bit difficult working with that racket thumping through the floorboards. I've been shouting at you for ages.'

What is it about parents? They ask you to follow an instruction and when you do what they want, instead of singing a hymn of thanks or organising a street party to celebrate, they spend the next half an hour going on about why it took you so *long* to do it.

Mum works for a big firm of architects. Unlike most of my friends' parents she blurs the distinction between work and home. When she's under any sort of pressure (which is most days), she brings a trail of architectural hassle into our house. Plus she hates commuting to town on the London Underground and is always moaning about it.

Don't get me wrong, she can be a top mum when she wants to be, and at times she offers brilliant support/ideas/cash. And when she's not too snowed under, I can really talk to her about important stuff. But her job drives me crazy. And, as if to pay me back for this stance, she carries around an industrial-sized bee in her bonnet about my passion for music.

She hadn't quite finished her doorway rant.

'If you put as much time into your schoolwork as the hours you spend with your records, you'd be a genius,' she complained.

I scowled at her.

'DJing isn't a job, Zoe.'

This second statement revealed a gaping hole in her knowledge of the music world and I was happy to put her right.

'DJing is a job for certain people,' I calmly explained to her. 'And, if you hadn't noticed, DJs are often extremely rich and famous. So, if someone's got to be a DJ, it might as well be yours truly.'

DJ Zed. That's me.

Of course, it's not my real name. To everyone else I'm Zoe Wynch, but if you want to make it as a top mixer you need a great stage name. In terms of my career, I've only actually ever done one gig. And that was my mate Becky's little sister's birthday party. All of the party-goers said I was great. But how seriously can you take a bunch of nine-year-olds?

Even though I sometimes seriously question my ability and have seen no prospects of landing my first 'proper' gig, I'm determined to make it. If 'Stubborn' were a middle name it would be mine. After I decide to do something, I really go for it. Sometimes this pays off, sometimes it doesn't. When I was a little kid this character trait used to drive Mum and Dad completely crazy. Whenever I was over-the-top stubborn, they used to call me 'Determined Dot'.

I remember one holiday. I must have been about five and we were heading for France. We were over halfway to the coast, when I realised I'd left my teddy, Frank, at home. I insisted pretty noisily that I wasn't going to cross the Channel unless Frank was with me. During this mind-blowing tantrum, my parents realised that if they didn't go home to get the damn thing, the next two weeks would be unbearable. 'Determined Dot' won that particular battle.

According to Dad, my stubbornness comes directly from Mum. He says we're more alike than either of us will ever accept. So arguments between Mum and me can be extremely hard to resolve. Neither of us wants to be the first to give in.

Dad's the one who got me into music. For as long as I can remember he encouraged me to explore his massive record collection and listen to as many different types of music as possible. When I was little I used to love arranging his records all over my bedroom floor and marvelling at the incredible colours and designs on the record sleeves. He's a professional bass player. And before anyone gets excited, he's not a multimillionaire or a glamorous celebrity with ten residences scattered across the globe. He was once semi-well-known, because he played for a moderately successful band in the Eighties called The Spiked Path. He was on TV a few times and got a couple of mug shots in the papers. But that was way back, when he and Mum were first together.

When they met he was a fresh-faced, excitable young musician and she was finishing her architecture degree at university. They bumped into each other after a gig he'd done at her student union. She was excited to meet someone creative and off-beat. He was delighted to chance upon someone who had a prospect of landing a 'proper' job one day. They got it together, bought a flat in Archway, had kids, and then moved to a house in Camden – our present abode.

When The Spiked Path became moderately unsuccessful, Dad began working as a session musician – playing bass for lots of different bands and singers. He's still at it – hanging out in studios and playing the odd live show. He sometimes complains that he's too old for it now, but I know he still really loves that whole scene. And he's been really encouraging about me and record mixing.

Mum's attitude towards my DJing, on the other hand, is very hostile. She's seen the ups and downs of the music biz through Dad's work. He can get a decent-sized cheque, then earn nothing for a few months. She's always been the one who earned the regular money. And that arrangement seems to work for them. However, when it comes to her daughter's future, she has this built-in terror that I'll end up penniless, living on old toast crumbs.

Sometimes Dad steps in and tells her to relax about the DJ thing, but she doesn't like these interventions, so he holds on to them for special occasions. Like when she really loses it.

Dad's into all kinds of music, but his favourite act of all time is The Three Degrees – a Seventies trio of sexy soul chanteuses.

'Great bass lines,' he says, when listening to any of their records, 'and fine-looking women as well.'

'What have their looks got to do with their music?' I once asked.

'Absolutely nothing,' he replied with an embarrassed grin. 'It just makes them interesting to watch on TV.'

Whenever he's a bit down, he slaps on a Three Degrees record and immediately says he feels a lot better. Sometimes I listen along with him. Their music was what first inspired me to start dipping into the 'soul' and 'disco' sections of his record collection, when I was about ten.

Then one day, when I heard someone at school talking about a radio station called CHILL FM, I began to tune in to it. CHILL started out as an illegal pirate station in north London, broadcasting to a few hundred people from a tiny flat in a giant tower block. By the time I'd caught wind of it, the station had got a licence, gone legal and was based in a building on Oxford Street. CHILL stuck with most of its original DJs and soon became the cutting-edge dance music station in the capital. There was one DJ who was particularly excellent – DJ Reel Love. He did (and still does) a brilliant show on Friday nights, with a great mix of well-known and rare tunes. As soon as I started to listen to him, I made up my mind that he was the greatest. I wanted to be him, or at least a female version of him.

Before long I was spending all of my pocket money buying twelve-inch records and playing them on Dad's old record player. Kids who came to our house viewed this machine as if it was some sort of ancient relic I'd unearthed during an archealogical dig. I have to say it did look funny – a battered old brown turntable with a chipped, see-through plastic lid – but I didn't care. I was listening to the finest music and dreaming about the day when I'd be able to afford some of my own equipment and play gigs in front of huge crowds of adoring fans.

In my quest to get near Reel Love (and with the help of my English teacher, Ms Devlin, whose brother knew someone who knew someone), I did a two-week work experience placement at CHILL at the start of this year's summer holidays. Mum wasn't crazy about this arrangement ('You shouldn't be cooped up inside a stuffy building all day in this weather'), but she let me do it anyway.

Beforehand, I was madly excited about the prospect of meeting Reel Love. I pictured myself in the centre of a room, surrounded by him, other DJs and loads of CHILL producers, who'd hang on to my every word and kill themselves with laughter at my witty anecdotes about the music industry.

Of course, it didn't work out quite like that.

For a start, Reel Love was in Ibiza the whole time I was there and someone I'd never heard of was covering his show. In addition, my work experience wasn't really connected to dance music in any way. I spent almost the entire two weeks between the coffee machine and the photocopier. After a few days of this, my brain was so squished that I started looking for milk in the paper tray. I didn't get anywhere near the DJs in spite of repeated attempts. The studios were on the third floor and were strictly out of bounds. I was in an office on the first floor. I did see a couple of them near the lifts, but one was having an argument on his mobile while the other was wearing huge headphones and rocking his head to some music. I decided against starting a conversation with either of them.

The one tiny upside of my two weeks at CHILL was meeting Jade Bell. She's a production assistant who works on several shows, including Reel Love's Friday night one. She's about twenty, with short, spiky blond hair and piercing blue eyes. She's very hard-working and wears a permanent frown on her face. I reckon she's either constantly unhappy or she's had facial surgery to remove her smile muscles. But I was absolutely set on befriending her. Surely, I decided, if I got matey with Jade then maybe I could get to meet Reel Love. And if I talked to him, maybe he'd pave the way for me to become a top DJ. I hadn't quite figured out how this would all work, but I pressed on with my plan regardless. 'Determined Dot' got stuck in.

For the two weeks, I was Miss Persistent, speaking to Jade whenever it was possible. I mentioned on my first day that Reel Love was my all-time hero, but I'm not sure she was listening properly because she was dialling a number on her phone and not looking at me as I was telling her this. When I tried on the second day, once again she didn't show any signs of hearing my declaration of love and respect for Reel Love. So I tried a different tack and started offering her my help. At the beginning of the second week, she did let me open a few letters and send some standard replies, but that was about it. When I went to say goodbye at the end of my work experience, she said, 'Remind me who you are again.'

OK, so I didn't make a huge impression on her, but I'm still working on it. As I was about to leave the building on my last day of work experience, one of the station managers asked me if I'd like to come in on Saturdays to help out. He stressed that there wouldn't be any money involved, but pointed out that I'd gain loads more experience. I didn't hesitate before saying yes – Reel Love would soon be back from Ibiza. Admittedly I wouldn't be around for his show and would probably never see him, but at least I'd be working in the same building as him.

I started a few weeks ago and that's where I can now be found between the hours of ten and five on Saturdays – striding between the coffee machine and the photocopier. And at least Jade knows my name now. She even used it when she asked me for a cup of coffee last week. And she used it again when she sent me back because I'd forgotten to put sugar in. Nothing to get too excited about. But it's a start.

* * *

Mum was still standing in the doorway, letting me know hostilities were far from over.

'Is there anything else?' I asked in my most patronising voice, the one teachers use when telling kids off.

'There's no need to be rude,' she snapped, hovering in the way that only parents do.

How do they achieve this effect? Have they got tiny air cushions on the soles of their shoes that make them levitate a few centimetres above the ground? My mind raced through all possible methods of getting her off my case and out of the room. Luckily, I didn't have to think for too long. The doorbell went.

'I'll get it,' I volunteered, feeling relieved. I sped past her down the stairs to open the door. It was my two best mates – Keesha and Becky.

I uttered a prayer of thanks and let them in.

When I started at Cahill Community School three years ago, I knew no one. All of my primary school friends had gone to Forrest Comp, but Mum persuaded Dad that a more 'academic' school would be better for me and somehow I got in to Cahill. It's a bit of a longer walk than to Forrest and my first impressions of the school weren't too promising.

By lunchtime on my third day at Cahill I'd decided that the next five years were going to be worse than a lifetime of solitary confinement in the world's grottiest prison. Then, thanks to what felt like a miracle, Keesha and Becky approached me in the playground that very lunchtime and we got chatting. They'd been friends with each other since nursery school but, for some reason, took me under their protective wing (they claimed it was because I seemed mysterious and interesting). So, instead of having to learn the ropes at Cahill by myself, I got to grips with everything in the company of those two.

Three years later and we're still a tight unit. They've watched my obsession with music grow and have encouraged me all the way, even though I know I sometimes bore them to death when I'm going on about mixes, slipmats and beats per minute.

'I'm sending you into a deep sleep,' I quip in my wackiest alien voice, whenever their eyes glaze over as I'm trying to explain the latest development in my obsession. This always makes them crack up with laughter.

Keesha is five foot five, with plaits, smoochy brown eyes and a great figure. She has a twenty-year-old sister, Amber, who's at Manchester University. Her parents are both lawyers with pretty high-powered jobs. Keesha is a human ball of vitality. She's the most positive person I've ever met and everyone loves her, especially boys – she makes everyone feel at ease. Sometimes she can be a bit too upbeat – some things in life are rubbish after all.

Becky's five foot three (same height as me), has amazing green eyes, long, straight jet black hair and a pointy nose. It was at Becky's sister Phoebe's ninth birthday party where I did my first DJ gig. Becky and Phoebe live with their mum. Their dad left soon after Phoebe was born, to 'find himself' in some 'Free Love Community'.

Becky's hilarious, quick-witted, fast-talking and incredibly bossy. One day she'll make a great parent, teacher or dictator.

We all like the same kinds of music. And films. And books. And TV shows. And people. However, when it comes to fashion and appearances, they both spend far longer on how they look than I ever will. Not that I don't care – I do. I want to look good. I just can't be bothered spending hours analysing myself in the mirror and years choosing what clothes to wear – not when there are records to be bought, listened to, and mixed.

I've got shoulder-length, straight blond hair and hazel eyes. My nose is tiny and sometimes I'm not sure whether I actually possess nostrils. I'm told I've got good legs, but they don't get out much. I'm not really a skirts kind of girl. Jeans, trainers and cool T-shirts are far more my style.

Keesha and Becky are always telling me I'm really pretty. And boys do seem to show me some attention. I find it pretty easy to talk to most people, but when it comes to talking to a boy I fancy (well one particular boy) my brain and my mouth disconnect and I find it hard to speak with recognisable words. So generally I keep my mouth shut.

As I ushered Keesha and Becky in, my mum swept thunderously downstairs. When she saw them, her expression softened a fraction and she managed a quick 'hello', before disappearing into the kitchen and slamming the door behind her.

'Trouble at the ranch?' whispered Keesha, as we went upstairs.

I did my best impression of a fire-breathing dragon and they both grinned.

'Music too loud again,' I said with a groan.

Keesha and Becky think I'm really funny. Making them laugh is one of my specialities.

We went into my room and flopped down on the bed.

Within a nanosecond, Keesha was chatting about Tim, a guy she met down in Devon during the summer. He's sixteen and a surfing fanatic. It's so un-Keesha to be heavily into a boy – usually it's the other way round. But with Tim things seem to be different.

'He's coming up to London on Sunday,' she said, pulling out a couple of photo-booth pictures of them together.

I shook my head and smiled. 'We know, Keesha. You've told us ten zillion times.'

She started listing all the places Tim was going to take her on their day of romance.

'The furthest Dan ever takes me is to Tony's Café,' Becky said with mock despair.

Becky's been going out with Dan for about six months. He's a really sweet guy in our year at school. But he's a bit in awe of her. Maybe that's because he can hardly ever get a word in. Becky definitely wears the trousers (and every other part of the outfit) in that relationship. As soon as she started going out with Dan, I knew I'd get on really well with him. He's a big music fan, as is his seventeen-year-old older brother, Howie (who's in the sixth form at Cahill and is trying to get into club promotion). Dan and I talk a lot about records and stuff. He informs me about obscure bands he's into and I tell him about my DJ hopes and dreams. Becky finds these conversations a complete snore and begs us to talk about something else.

Keesha has Tim. Becky has Dan. That leaves me. No boyfriend. No signs of getting one. I have gone out with boys before, but each time it only lasted a couple of weeks and the boys were more into me than I was into them. However, there is one boy I'm completely crazy about. He's called Josh Stanton and I noticed him in my first week at Cahill.

Josh has got short brown hair that he gels at the front (creating a gorgeous spiky effect), magnetic silvery-blue eyes to die for, and one of the most beautiful smiles I've ever had the pleasure to drool over. He's about five foot nine and is in really good shape. He's good at several sports, but he's not one of those boys who take themselves too seriously. He's also into acting and had a small part in the school play last year. I, of course, went to see it on all three nights.

One of the problems concerning the object of my affections is that I've hardly ever spoken to him. He's in the year above us at school, so his timetable is completely different from ours. In fact, the most complex sentence I've uttered to him is probably, 'Hi.' Plus, there are only so many times you can just 'happen' to be in the same place at the same time as someone else without being jailed for stalking. And, anyway, even when I do appear he never seems to be aware of my presence.

Becky must have been reading my mind.

'Still pining for Josh?' she enquired.

'Oh the pain of unrequited love,' I replied forlornly.

'Come on, Zoe,' said Keesha, 'we've been over this time and time again. He might be totally into you. You don't know because you've never asked him.'

'Yeah right,' I answered. 'So all I need to do is go up to him and say, "You don't really know me, Josh, but I've had a crush on you for three years and was just wondering, on the off chance, if you fancied me?"'

'Something like that,' said Keesha, laughing, 'but maybe a bit less direct.'

'Anyway,' I sighed, 'it's too late. He's started going out with Gail Simmonds.'

Gail is our year's supermodel – sparkling white teeth, strawberry blond hair and a set of boobs so 'out there' that, as well as ensnaring boys, they can probably perform a range of other tricks, like reading maps or conducting an orchestra.

'It's only a rumour,' said Becky.

'Why don't we forget about Josh for a minute,' suggested Keesha. 'There are plenty of other boys out there who fancy you.'

'Name one,' I challenged her.

Keesha's silence failed to reassure me.

'They haven't identified themselves yet,' Becky said quickly. 'They're just waiting for the right moment.'

Before I could take this argument any further, there was a knock at my door and my brother Zak walked in.

I often ask myself, where were the other twenty-five letters of the alphabet when my parents named us? Zoe and Zak? What were they thinking of? Did they want us to grow up and become a double-act on kids TV? It used to annoy me a bit, especially when other kids taunted us about it, but now it doesn't bother me at all.

Zak's sixteen and is at sixth-form college. He's everything you could want an older brother to be. He's always on hand to offer decent advice. He puts up with all of my gripes and moans. I talk to him about most things, but he knows nothing of my infatuation with Josh. I just can't bring myself to discuss it with him. Even though he's a good listener, I'm worried he might not take me seriously.

Most importantly, Zak laughs at my jokes. He's tall, wiry, and any kind of clothes seem to look good on him. He's got cropped blond hair and his eyes are exactly like mine. He's no model, but loads of girls fall for his mischievous grin and cheeky personality. Mum says Zak's exactly like Dad was when she first met him – 'a charmer'.

Unfortunately for the girls in his life, he isn't into commitment of any sort. He's quite up front about 'playing the field'. So however much any girl might want him to be a 'serious' boyfriend, he doesn't make empty promises. As a result he's always got several girls on the go.

The funny thing is that, in spite of all this girl attention, Zak's not at all arrogant. He's genuinely amazed that so many females are interested in him. I'm constantly laughing with him about his lack of interest in long-term relationships. In short, he's a great guy to have as a brother – I just wouldn't recommend him to anyone as a boyfriend.

'Hi Keesha, hi Becky,' he said, smiling. He sat down on the chair opposite my bed.

'So who's the present love of Zak Wynch's life?' asked Keesha.

'I'm sort of going out with Laura Tanner,' he replied, stroking his chin.

Laura's in the sixth form at Cahill – she's a year older than Zak. She's very pretty – a petite blonde with crystal-clear blue eyes.

'Sort of?' asked Becky.

'It's just that there's this great girl at college called Iman,' he explained.

'Shame on you,' said Becky, laughing.

'You're going to get yourself in big trouble one day,' added Keesha, trying to look disapproving, but grinning instead.

He didn't have time to respond to these observations because the front door bell rang and, a second later, Mum shouted upstairs.

'Zak, Laura's here to see you.'

He stood up and, as he walked over to the door, his mobile rang. He answered it.

'Hi Claire,' he said softly. He listened for a few seconds and then spoke again.

'Tonight's great. About eight o'clock. See you then.'

He flipped his mobile shut, beamed at us and left the room to see Laura.

'Unbelievable,' mouthed Keesha.

'Remarkable,' whispered Becky.

'Seen it all before,' I said, groaning.

Becky looked at her watch.

'Come on,' she said, jumping up from the bed enthusiastically. 'We're meeting Dan and some of his mates at the park in ten minutes. Let's go.'

Keesha got up and she and Becky walked over to the door. I stayed firmly rooted to the bed. There were two new records I'd bought yesterday that were crying out for a spin, if Mum relented about the noise. I'd blown the last few dregs of my allowance on them and they needed me.

'Come on, Zoe, it'll be a laugh,' Keesha urged.

'Josh Stanton might be there,' added Becky.

With that, I leaped up as if propelled by an uncurling spring.

'Excuse me?' I asked, my eyes wide with surprise.

'Dan's got a bit friendly with him recently,' she said. 'They're playing in some football team together.'

'Why didn't you tell me before?' I demanded.

'I only found out this morning.'

This could be interesting. Maybe their friendship would give me a chance to get a tiny bit closer to Josh.

My momentary excitement though was suddenly shrouded in doubt.

'What happens if he's there with Gail?' I asked.

'He won't be,' said Becky. 'I told you, it's just a rumour.'

I stood up hesitantly and followed them, throwing one last loving glance at my system.

Downstairs, we could hear Mum in the kitchen, participating in a heated phone exchange.

'I said it'll be there on time,' she barked, 'so it'll be there on time!'

We walked down and I poked my head round the kitchen door. Mum was holding the receiver and looking frazzled.

'I'm going to the park with Keesha and Becky to see some mates,' I whispered. 'Back by seven.'

She nodded and gave me a quick wave.

Mum's very hot on getting-home times. We have an understanding. If I say I'll be back by a certain hour, this time is set in stone. If this time changes for any reason, I phone her. Failure to comply with this arrangement means my life is effectively over.

We left the house and headed for the park. As we walked down the street, my mind started racing. Could today be the day that Josh suddenly notices me, sweeps me into his arms and passionately declares that I'm the girl for him?

It didn't take long for me to come up with the answer.

It's about as likely as you becoming a fish, I told myself.

And remember, you're a terrible swimmer.

Chapter 2 . Love Struck

There's another central figure in my life. Her name is Tania Trent. She's twenty-five, tall and slim, with a blond, perfectly shaped bob haircut, shiny green eyes and immaculately manicured nails.

Oh yes. The other thing about Tania: she isn't real. And before anyone accuses me of having an imaginary friend, I can put that little idea to rest. She's not a friend – she's a professional contact.

I did have an imaginary friend when I was four. She was called Molly and I insisted on doing all the things that kids do with their imaginary friends. I made Mum and Dad set a place for her at the table. I included Molly in all of my games, even if it meant I sometimes lost. I demanded that wherever we went she came with us.

But when I started having tantrums for Molly as well as myself, Mum and Dad sent her packing. One morning they told me she'd gone to live somewhere else. And, even though Molly was my imaginary friend, for some reason I believed them. I was heartbroken for days and it cost them quite a few packets of chocolate buttons to help me get over it.

So Tania isn't some kid's mealtime mate, she's what I call a 'Virtual Ally'. She's a TV presenter working on a programme called *Daytime Living*. The studio in which the programme is recorded is draped in soft shades of blue and yellow. There are two sofas, a low-level glass coffee table and some exotic plants on the floor. A light mauve backdrop declares the name of the programme. And, although episodes of *Daytime Living* play out solely in my head, they always seem so real.

I'm often a guest on the show and Tania is brilliant at inflating my ego, especially when events in my life aren't going according to plan. Like my trip to the park with Keesha and Becky. I stood around for ages, trying to talk to Dan and his friends, but I was constantly checking out every pathway to see if Josh Stanton was approaching. He never showed. I made an appearance on *Daytime Living* the following morning during one of Ms Devlin's English lessons:

Tania: *So Zoe, I hear that your little rendezvous with movie super-star Ricky Dance didn't quite take place.*
Zoe: *You're absolutely right, Tania. I was told he might be there, but it was a no show. I got totally fed up waiting for him. I heard he turned up well after I was gone.*
Tania: *Do you think he was disappointed at missing you?*
Zoe: *Disappointed? He was totally and absolutely distraught. He phoned me, texted me, e-mailed me, faxed me, and apparently even*

tried to contact me via carrier pigeon. Then first thing this morning I got a delivery of fifty red roses. The note with them said: From Ricky. Can you ever forgive me? I'll do whatever it takes.

Tania: And have you called to thank him?

Zoe: No way! I'll keep him guessing. Nothing makes up for being stood up.

Tania: So where does that leave your love life?

Zoe: I'm glad you asked, Tania, because, as Ricky's flowers were arriving, the phone went. It was Guy Spencer.

Tania: Not the Guy Spencer, Ricky's great film-star rival?

Zoe: The very same. He said he was dying to meet me and had put everything else in his life on hold until I agreed to see him.

Tania: And how did you respond to that?

Zoe: I said he'd have to fit in with my extremely busy schedule.

Tania: But isn't he shooting a movie at the moment?

Zoe: Yes he is. But he's locked himself up in his apartment to wait for me to say yes. Word is, his director and the rest of the film crew are going crazy.

Tania: So when will you get back to him?

Zoe: All in good time, Tania. I'll have to check out my other offers first. There are so many, I'm not sure I'll have time to consider them all properly. Mind you, Ricky's roses do look great in my kitchen.

'Well, Zoe?'

Visions of Ricky and Guy suddenly evaporated into the ether as Ms Devlin's voice brought me grinding back to reality.

Ms Devlin's OK. She's about twenty-seven, which is on the extremely young side compared to most of the other teachers at Cahill. I'm sure some of them have actually died, but the school can't be bothered to get rid of them. Ms Devlin makes an effort with her appearance – which sets her apart as a fashion icon in the staff room. And Keesha, Becky and I have seen her boyfriend. He picked her up one day after school on his motorbike. We agreed unanimously that he was pretty good-looking in a grungy, biker kind of way. I'm also hugely grateful to her for helping me get my foot in the door at CHILL.

We were nearing the end of an English lesson about Shakespeare's *Othello*.

'Sorry?' I asked hesitantly.

'What was Iago's motivation?' she asked.

'Iago's motivation,' I replied slowly, playing for time.

'Yes, Zoe,' she said, as a hint of impatience crept into her usually laid-back voice. 'This is the third time I've asked you.'

Before her positive personality turned sour, a winged angel landed on my desk. It took the form of a scribbled piece of paper in Keesha's handwriting. I scanned it quickly.

'He was jealous of Othello's power and wanted to turn him against Desdemona,' I stated with authority.

'Thank you, Zoe.' Ms Devlin nodded as her frown transformed back to a smile. 'Good answer, even if it did take you a while to get there.'

She was about to ask me another question, but she ran out of time. Thirty of us herded towards the door like wildebeest, a second after the bell rang.

'Slowly!' she called as we streamed out.

As soon as we were halfway along the corridor, I flung my arms around Keesha and gave her a massive hug.

'Easy tiger,' she said laughing, as I nearly squeezed the life out of her.

I let go and leaned back against a row of lockers.

'Brilliant work Keesha,' said Becky, grinning, 'and you sounded so confident, Zoe. Pretty impressive, considering you haven't read one page of it.'

On Sunday morning I did try and read a few pages of *Othello*, just in case Ms Devlin decided to question me further the next day. But I kept putting it down and turning to my monthly DJ bible, *In the Mix* – a bit more interesting than a sixteenth-century play written in a weird language that only bears a passing resemblance to English. *In the Mix* had a special feature on Reel Love and I was reading it for the fifth time. I'd been really worked off my feet at CHILL the day before. I spent so much time by the photocopier that I was thinking of moving in with it when I leave home.

The Wynch household on Sunday mornings is a tranquil environment. It's pyjamas in the kitchen, the weekend paper, coffee and mounds of toast. Zak was reading the sports section, Mum was locked into a news story and Dad was devouring the gardening pages. There was a knock at the front door. We all looked at the kitchen clock. Who would dream of turning up on a Sunday at eleven-thirty in the morning?

No one moved.

'All right, all right,' I exclaimed dramatically, getting up from my chair. 'Don't trouble yourselves.'

Mum, Dad and Zak had already returned to their sections of the paper as I stamped down the hall to open the front door.

It was Becky.

'Hi.' She nodded in a business-like manner, stepping into the house. 'We're on a mission.'

'What kind of mission?' I asked.

'I'll tell you on the way,' she replied.

'Give me two minutes,' I said.

I ran upstairs to my room and pulled on my faded jeans, long-sleeved purple T-shirt, hooded white fleece and trainers.

By the time I got down, Becky was sitting in the kitchen, having a piece of toast and talking to Zak. On seeing me she put her half-nibbled toast down and hurried me towards the front door.

'What's going on?' I demanded as we headed up the street.

'We're meeting Keesha,' she told me. 'Tim's not coming up to London today. He dumped her.'

'You're joking!' I said, shocked. 'No one has ever finished with Keesha.'

'It gets worse,' she continued. 'He didn't even have the guts to phone her. He did it by e-mail – told her he's met some eighteen-year-old Australian girl. Said he and Keesha are strictly past tense.'

'No way!' I stammered.

Becky nodded and we sped up.

We found Keesha in Tony's Café, thumbing through an old copy of *Cosmo* and miserably sipping from a can of Coke.

Tony's is just off Camden High Street and is really old-fashioned. It's got booths backed in peeling red leather and most of the food options have seen far better days. So it's always strictly a drinks stop for us. Keesha looked up when we came in. Her eyes were rimmed with red and her skin looked blotchy.

Keesha crying over a boy! In the world news stakes this was just one rung below Martians opening a bakery on the High Street.

'Thanks for coming, guys,' Keesha said and sniffed. She picked a napkin off the table to wipe her eyes. Becky sat next to her and put her arm round her. I sat on the opposite bench and reached out my hand. Keesha took it in both of hers.

'Look at me,' she said quietly. 'I can't believe he's made me feel like this.'

She stopped talking as more tears streamed down her cheeks.

'But Keesha,' I said, 'you're the number one catch in the country.'

'If not the world,' Becky agreed.

Keesha managed a weak smile and grabbed another napkin.

'You two are top mates,' she said, drying her eyes again. 'I don't know what I'd do without you. I didn't want to trouble Amber – she's got enough on her plate at uni. And there's no way I'm going to discuss it with Mum and Dad.'

'That's why we're here,' I said with a grin. 'Try getting rid of us.'

'I really liked him,' Keesha murmured, wiping her eyes.

'We know,' I said, squeezing her hands.

Becky and I spent over an hour telling Keesha why Tim had just blown one of the world's most golden opportunities. We'd succeeded in cheering her up a fraction when Becky's face suddenly brightened.

'How about we go for some retail therapy?' she suggested. 'Take your mind off things?'

Keesha was doubtful at first, but Becky can sell humps to a camel. A few minutes later we were striding down Camden High Street, heading for Girl Trend – Keesha's favourite shop. I was more than happy to join this jaunt, but I'd be going as a mere onlooker rather than a purchaser. Cash flow was a bit of a problem. Basically, there was hardly any cash and definitely no flow. I'd blown all of my savings on my DJ gear and my allowance had only stretched a few days as I'd spent it on records. The couple of pound coins in my purse represented my entire financial worth. Plus none of the clothes there were really my style.

Girl Trend is all low lighting, glitz and shimmer – very Keesha. We walked inside and stepped through its darkened interiors. Keesha was reluctant to go in at first, but we gave her another pep talk and eventually she wiped her eyes and pulled a defiant expression.

'OK,' she declared, 'I'm going in. And I'm going to buy something outrageous.'

'Way to go girl!' shouted Becky as Keesha disappeared into the maze of clothes racks. Becky and I followed her in.

A few minutes later, Keesha called us over to one of the changing booths. She emerged sporting a skimpy blue and green tartan miniskirt. Her eyes didn't look so puffy any more and the skirt looked superb. Becky and I nodded approvingly. Keesha bought the skirt and, as we left Girl Trend, her mood seemed to have lifted.

'Thanks for being brilliant,' she said gratefully. 'It's just been such a shock.'

'No problem,' I said, nudging her arm.

We were halfway up the High Street, arms linked together, when I saw them.

Becky had seen them too and tried to steer us in the direction of a bookshop on the other side of the street. But it was too late. We were about two metres away from a bus stop when my feet suddenly refused to move.

It was Josh and Gail. They were standing inside the bus shelter. Snogging.

So the rumour was true – they were together. What a great way to find out. They were really at it. Gail looked like she was about to eat his face. I stood rooted to the spot, staring at this devastating scene.

'Come on, Zoe,' Becky urged, dragging me across the road.

I was motionless and speechless.

'If I'm going to get over Tim, you've got to forget about Josh,' said Keesha firmly, abruptly changing from comforted to comforter.

I wanted to point out that in all probability, Keesha would never see Tim again, whereas I would be forced to see Josh and Gail all over the place.

Surely the world has just ended, I thought to myself.

Keesha and Becky managed to get me across the street, but my eyes were firmly fixed on Josh and Gail. They were getting on to a bus, holding hands and laughing.

'Come on,' Becky implored me, pulling me towards the bookshop.

We walked inside and when I turned round to look back one more time, the bus had gone.

Chapter 3 . Playing in Tune

Some people (like my mum) look at DJs and think, Big deal, so they play a few records. How skilful is that? There's no real talent involved. Anyone could do it.

If only they knew how much work went into becoming a half-decent mixer.

Say you're DJing in a club. It's totally packed and the crowd are dancing euphorically. One of your headphones is perched behind one ear, letting you listen to the track that's coming out of the speakers on Deck 1. The other headphone is covering the other ear, allowing you to work privately with the record on Deck 2. You're moving this new track backward and forward on a slipmat, under the needle, finding the exact place you want to 'cut it in' and making sure it'll play in time with the first record. You may need to speed it up or slow it down. If you spend too long lining up the second record, the first one could finish and you'll be left with a gaping silence. And when it comes to a DJ set, gaping silences aren't recommended.

As you're trying to do all that, there's the sound of the crowd to contend with – not to mention the people who approach you with requests for their favourite song from ten years ago.

If you're working the decks properly, you use your cross fader on the mixing desk to bring in the second tune – this is the part where it gets really exciting. Sometimes you do this quickly and change tracks almost instantly. It's sharp. It's dramatic. But at other times you do a gradual fade, so that both tracks are playing together for a while. When you want to lose the first track, you fade it out using the up fader connected to Deck 1 (they're called 'up faders', even though you use them to fade music up and down). You increase the volume on the second track by using the up fader for Deck 2.

The idea behind this process is to achieve a seamless mix – the very best DJs make it almost impossible to tell where one record ends and another begins. When you listen to someone as good as Reel Love, it sounds like his whole set is one continuous tune.

So you're doing a set in this club and it lasts an hour. That's quite a few mixes to get in and each one has to be perfect. When a mix goes wrong, the noise you create is truly awful. But when you get things right, it sounds incredible.

So in case anyone like my mum does ask – *that's* the big deal. It might look simple, but get someone in off the street and ask them to mix two records, and you'll soon be diving for your earplugs.

* * *

I'd been talking to Zak over breakfast about a new track I'd heard
the night before on CHILL. It was a Wednesday morning and he
wasn't really up for a musical lecture so, as soon as he sensed I'd
finished, he bolted for the front door and out to the other side of
our street, where Laura Tanner was waiting for him. I was about
to leave for school when the phone rang.

'Is Zak there?' asked a female voice.

'He's not in,' I replied.

'Oh.'

'Do you want me to give him a message?'

'No, it's OK. My name's Iman. I'm at college with him and I was
wondering where he is. He's normally here by now.'

'He left about five minutes ago,' I told her, omitting the fact that
I could see him that very minute, smooching with Laura before
they parted and he walked to college while she went to school.

'It's just that I've been trying his mobile,' Iman continued, 'and
it's switched off.'

'I'm sure he'll be there soon,' I told her.

'Thanks,' she replied.

I hung up.

Like I said, Zak's a great guy. But boyfriend material – forget it.

I nipped out to Tune Spin at lunchtime.

It was over a week since the bus stop sighting of Josh and Gail.
Whenever I thought of them snogging, I felt completely destroyed.

Despite my efforts in school to avoid them, I had spotted them together a couple of times, looking very loved up.

So I reckoned spending my free time poring over records (even though I couldn't afford any) might be a good alternative to mooning around like an abandoned dog and driving Keesha and Becky insane. Plus, checking out twelve-inches almost always cheered me up.

Tune Spin is a record store under the arches of a railway bridge behind the High Street. It's half the size of all the other shops in the area. Its roof is made of corrugated iron and its wooden front door hangs slightly off its hinges. Inside, the walls are covered in posters advertising new releases, flyers promoting upcoming gigs and photos of legendary DJs.

I'm convinced that Rix, the sole employee of Tune Spin, must be up for the Most Patronising Creep in the Universe Award. When I started going there, I understandably presumed that the person who worked there would be a font of great musical knowledge and an inspirational figure in my quest to become a DJ. On entering the shop for the first time, I asked Rix about a record I'd heard on CHILL a couple of days previously. He looked up from the magazine he was studying, sneered at me and then returned to his reading matter. I asked the question again only slightly louder this time, which prompted him to slam the magazine down and tell me he'd never heard of it.

And that's the way he's behaved towards me ever since – unavailable, unhelpful, and unpleasant. At first I thought his blatant rudeness was down to the fact that I was only fourteen and he reckoned I was just some 'kid'. But the more I went in, the more I understood that his attitude was down to my being a girl. When boys my age (or even younger) visited the shop, Rix was only too happy to conduct an in-depth chat with them or make a huge effort to locate a record they were after.

But this realisation just made me more determined to hang out there. 'Determined Dot' would be a regular visitor to the shop, if only to annoy Rix.

Rix is tall, thin and pale with three earrings in his left ear and a straggly brown goatee beard hanging from his chin. Despite visiting Tune Spin on countless occasions, the only things I've ever managed to find out about him (gleaned from snippets of overheard conversations with other customers) are: he's seventeen; he doesn't own the shop – it's owned by someone called Dave who spends most of the year in Spain; he fancies himself a top DJ.

The decks, mixer and speakers in Tune Spin are first class – far better than anything I could afford. When Rix isn't monopolising the system (he loves showing off to anyone who'll listen), some customers try out new twelve-inches on these decks. Since I got my system I've approached the Tune Spin decks twice when Rix has been chatting to someone or banging around in the back of the shop. But each time I've backed away at the last minute, fearing he'd appear and turn it into a public humiliation.

Rix was standing behind me and looking over my shoulder at the rack of American imports I was flicking through.

'Way out of your league,' he muttered.

I ignored him and carried on picking out various records and studying their sleeve notes.

'I think they're a bit too sophisticated for you,' he told me. 'Leave them to the real DJs.'

'Go away,' I said, feeling myself blushing.

'How about coming back when Daddy gives you some more pocket money?' he added, looking around as if searching for someone to share these hilarious words of mockery. But we were the only people in the shop.

He ambled off to the mixer and I watched sideways as he dropped two records on to the decks and pulled on some headphones. A few seconds later, there was a rare seventies disco tune pumping out of the speakers. He smirked across at me as if waiting for me to applaud him. I turned away and continued my fantasy shopping spree. I wandered around the shop for five more minutes, then checked my watch and went. As I left, he was fading in another Seventies dance track and grinning to himself smugly.

Back at school I found Keesha and Becky in the toilets, with five minutes to go before the afternoon's history lesson. Keesha was trying out a couple of different lip-glosses. Becky was acting as her personal stylist and was also slapping her on the back, congratulating her.

'What's the celebration for?' I asked.

'Keesha has only just sent the finest e-mail in history,' said Becky, grinning.

'Who to?' I asked.

'Tim,' Keesha explained. 'I thought I'd tell him how to treat a girl properly.'

'Nice one,' I said, smiling.

'We came looking for you to help us write it,' said Becky, 'but you weren't around. Bet you were at Tune Spin with the charming Rix.'

I nodded. I often moan to them about my encounters with Rix and his rudeness.

'Buy anything?' asked Keesha.

I shook my head. 'No funds,' I replied.

'Once you hit the big time,' said Becky, 'you can buy the whole shop and sack Rix.'

We all laughed and walked out to the corridor. We were halfway to our lesson when whispers started rushing along the corridor, at the speed of a bushfire.

'Mad Max is coming. Mad Max is coming.'

Jeffrey Maxwell is our head teacher. He's a massive man, with huge shoulders, fleshy ears, grey eyes and a well-trimmed beard. I thought you had to like kids, even just a tiny little bit, to become a teacher, but an affinity for children was definitely not in Mad Max's job description. He's been at Cahill for five years and makes it quite clear that, if any of his pupils stray even a few millimetres out of line, they'll be banished from his school before they can squeal 'discipline problems'. Everyone at Cahill without exception is, at the very least, wary of Mad Max and, at the most, downright terrified of the man. When he's on the prowl it's best to stay out of his way.

We watched his towering figure march into view, with kids scattering in front of him like terrified mice desperately trying to escape from a wildcat. He paced along the corridor telling people the lunch break was over and that it was time to get to their class-rooms. He strode towards us and we stood to one side to let him pass. But to our shock and dismay he stopped right next to us, glowering.

'Zoe Wynch?' he barked at me.

The other kids in the corridor watched in a stupefied trance. Keesha and Becky were glued to my sides, looking on with horror.

'Yes, Mr Maxwell,' I whispered.

He stared at me for what must have been ten seconds but felt like a couple of centuries and then spoke again, pronouncing each word very carefully as if sentencing someone to death.

'My office. Eight-thirty tomorrow morning.'

Chapter 4 • Who Gave You Permission to Come Into My Room?

I needed Zak's advice. When I got home the house was quiet. This was great in one way, as I didn't want Mum or Dad overhearing anything about tomorrow's meeting with Mad Max. But it was bad in another way, because Zak was out. I tried his mobile but it was switched off, so I dumped my school bag on my bed and went in search of a snack from the kitchen. As I ate a cream cheese sandwich with gherkin slices, I went over every possible reason for Mad Max wanting to see me. Even using the cleverest parts of my brain, I drew a complete blank and phoned Keesha.

'It's driving me mad,' I told her. 'What's it all about?'

'No idea,' she replied, 'but there's no point in you sitting at home, worrying about it alone. I'll phone Becky and we'll meet you at Tony's.'

'Maybe I'm going to be expelled,' I said as we ordered coffees twenty minutes later.

'For what?' asked Becky. 'Failing to conform to Mad Max's fashion sense?'

'He might want to present you with an award for the Most Focused Listener in Ms Devlin's class,' Keesha mused.

We all burst out laughing.

Then suddenly I stopped laughing and frowned. 'Come on, I'm serious.'

'Maybe it's a mistake,' said Keesha, 'Mad Max might have got you mixed up with someone else.'

This was a non-starter. When it came to dressing downs, Mad Max knew exactly who his targets were. The guy was a professional.

After an hour of discussion, none of us had come up with any logical reason for my summons, so I stood up.

Keesha looked surprised. 'You can't go yet,' she pleaded. 'We haven't got anywhere.'

'I'm not prepared to stay in Tony's all night,' I replied. 'It'll just have to wait till the morning.'

'Just another half-hour,' said Becky. 'Even if we can't figure it out, I need to stay away from home as long as possible. Phoebe's driving me absolutely mad at the minute. She's only nine for God's sake, but she keeps wanting me to lend her things.: Make-up. Clothes. A personality.'

I pulled a half-smile. 'Thanks for the help girls, but I'm off.'

'What are you going to do?' asked Keesha.

'I need to get a bit of mixing in.'

Their faces instantly adopted that 'Please spare us the musical details' expression. They both promised they'd ring me later if they had any new ideas. But I wouldn't be waiting by the phone.

On my way home, I popped into the Store Room. It's the kind of shop that sells absolutely everything. I picked up a funky-looking folder that the coins in my purse would just stretch to. In my head I was going over which tunes I'd spin first when I got home. I'd just reached the top of the fruit and veg aisle when I suddenly stopped. There standing in front of the newspaper and magazine section was Josh Stanton. He was thumbing through a football mag and looked totally engrossed in it. I stood there for a few seconds, staring at him. He was so good-looking and his gelled-up hair looked incredibly cute.

Why did I have to choose him? The boy was in the super good-looking league. Even if I had a complete facial make-over including a nose-lengthening operation, there was no way he'd ever go for me.

I felt a nudge in my side as a young couple tried to steer their shopping trolley round the girl with the crazy staring eyes and the open mouth. I quickly snapped out of my trance and grabbed the nearest item, which happened to be some broccoli. I held it up to shield my face, in case Josh turned round and saw me gawping at him. I stood there for a few seconds, peeking out from behind the green foliage. For a couple of seconds, I felt the urge to cast off my inhibitions, stride right up to Josh and give him an enormous kiss.

There were, however, certain problems with that strategy. A) He probably just wanted to read his magazine and not be interrupted by a kissogram carrying broccoli. B) He might be horrified and call security. C) He had a girlfriend.

'Zoe.'

I spun round.

Gail Simmonds was standing behind me – the person in the world I most wanted *not* to see me. She stood there, looking at me with a puzzled expression. My cheeks turned a deep shade of red.

Oh my God! How long had she been there? Did she know I'd been watching Josh? Was she about to cause me monumental embarrassment?

To divert her attention from my flushed face, I quickly smelled the broccoli and nodded wisely.

'Lovely and fresh,' I said, before picking up a large cauliflower.

Lovely and fresh! When did I become Greengrocer of the Year?

'What's up?' she asked.

Had she or hadn't she seen me spying on him?

'Just buying some fruit and vegetables,' I babbled.

'That's interesting,' she said without interest.

My brain had to work fast to get the next lie out.

'It's my dad's birthday and I'm cooking a meal for him.'

Possibly convincing?

'That's very sweet of you,' she said condescendingly.

Calm down, Zoe. She didn't see you. If she had, she'd have said something by now. She has no idea you're crazy about Josh. She won't have made any connections.

'OK,' she said.

'Right,' I replied awkwardly.

Without warning she suddenly called out, 'Josh!'

He looked up from his magazine and slowly replaced it in the rack and started to walk over in our direction.

I needed to make a sharp exit.

'Got to go,' I explained. 'It'll take me ages to make the meal.'

'See you,' she said.

Josh was only a few metres away and was advancing fast. I smiled at Gail and hurried off, back down the fruit and veg aisle. It was a lucky escape, but it could have been cringingly awful. I hurried to the checkout.

When I got in, Zak was in the hallway about to go out.

'How's it going?' he asked, putting his jacket on.

'It's madness,' I replied. 'Are Mum and Dad in?'

'Dad's playing on some gospel thing in town but Mum's about. Something went wrong with her computer at work. She lost loads of stuff and for some stupid reason hadn't backed any of it up. She's in a foul mood, so stay clear.'

'Where are you off to?' I enquired.

'Seeing Laura. Might go to a film.'

He peered inside the blue and white plastic bag I was carrying.

'Why have you got a broccoli and a cauliflower?'

I waved the question away. 'Far too complicated,' I explained, 'but just before you go I need to tell you something.'

I quickly informed him about the Mad Max summons.

'And you've got no idea what it's about?' he asked, looking a trifle concerned.

I shook my head and whispered, 'No, and not a word to Mum and Dad.'

'What do you think I am?' he asked me.

'OK, OK,' I replied.

'Have you been in trouble?' he asked.

'No.'

'Have you been bunking off?'

'No.'

'Have you hit anyone?'

'No.'

'So don't worry about it,' he said. 'It's probably nothing.'

A trip to Mad Max's office is never nothing.

He said goodbye and went out to get Laura.

I tiptoed upstairs. The light under the door of Mum's study was on and I hurried past. She'd probably be up half the night, cursing her work computer, bubbling with rage and frustration. I opened my bedroom door and was greeted by a rather unpleasant sight.

Far from struggling with an unforgiving deadline, Mum was sitting on my bed. My school stuff was arranged in a fan shape in front of her. She was flicking through the pages of my English book.

'What's going on?' I demanded suspiciously.

She closed the book and looked at me with a 'serious mother' expression.

'I'm just going through your work,' she told me.

'I can see that,' I replied. 'The question is who gave you permission to come into my room and snoop? I'm fourteen, not four!'

'I'm not snooping and I don't need permission to come in. All I'm doing is checking everything's OK.'

'Everything is OK.'

'Well then surely you don't have a problem with me looking.'

'I don't look through your work.'

'Don't be facetious.'

Why do parents use flash words to defend their actions? Do they really think we don't understand them?

'What does facetious mean?'

Mum raised her eyes to the ceiling. I stamped my foot on the floor like a toddler.

'Why don't you wait till Open Evening to check out my work?' I hissed, 'like every other parent on the planet. And in case you hadn't noticed, there isn't an Open Evening tonight. Unless there's a bunch of teachers hiding in my cupboard.'

She didn't laugh at my incredible wit.

'Calm down, Zoe,' she said slowly.

That's another trick parents use. They wind their kids up and then tell them to calm down.

'I am calm,' I said through gritted teeth.

'Well, all I can say is that I'm pleased I came in here.'

'What's that supposed to mean?'

'It's your work, Zoe.'

'What about it?'

'It's not . . . it's not as good as it used to be.'

'What are you talking about?'

'Your standards have definitely slipped.'

Her words hung in the air for a few seconds as I tried to think of a reply. But she got in first.

'I'm sure it's connected to you buying that DJ equipment. I should never have said yes to it.'

'Not this again!' I complained.

But she was in full flow by now.

'I'm worried that DJing is taking over your life. It's fine to have hobbies, but when you spend more time on them than your school work, then something's wrong. I think your work would be much better if you cut down on the time you spend with your records.'

Hobbies? Had the woman completely taken leave of her senses?

I tried very hard to sound relaxed.

'Have any of my teachers complained about my work?'

This is always a good fight-back strategy – ask a question with an answer you know helps your cause. It puts any parent momentarily off their stride.

She was momentarily put off her stride.

'There you go then,' I said. 'We've been back a few weeks. If anyone was going to make a fuss they'd have done it by now.'

'That's not the point, Zoe.'

'Of course it's the point!' I insisted, raising my voice. 'Teachers are the ones who are responsible for my education, not you!'

'Sometimes teachers don't have enough time to look properly at your work. They mean well, but they've got hundreds of other books to mark. All I'm saying is that your work is suffering because of your DJing.'

'That's rubbish,' I said. 'I keep my music totally separate from school work. I'm not at my decks all the time. And I'm doing fine at school.'

Mum shook her head and turned back to my books. She opened my English book again. A deeply disturbing thought sprang into my mind.

Maybe this wasn't the first time she'd checked out my work. Maybe she'd been spying on me for ages. How else would she know if my standards had slipped?

And then suddenly it hit me.

This was what tomorrow was about – the summons from Mad Max. It was down to Mum. She must have contacted him about her DJ/schoolwork concerns and asked him to give me a lecture.

I glared at her furiously, armed with this new information. I walked over to my bed and snatched my English book out of her hands. The cover ripped off as I wrenched it away.

'How dare you!' she snapped.

But I was in no mood for civilised behaviour.

'How dare YOU?' I shouted. 'Why didn't you talk to me first?'

I couldn't believe it. My own mum going to Mad Max behind my back.

'I am talking to you,' she replied, 'at least I'm trying to.'

But I was already halfway out of my bedroom, clutching the ripped English book to my chest as if it was a vulnerable newborn chick. She called after me to come back, but I stomped off downstairs.

This time she'd really crossed the line. Using Mad Max to reinforce her stupid attitude about my DJing was way over the top.

I grabbed my mobile and keys off the kitchen table and yanked open the front door. I walked up to the nearest lamp-post and rang Keesha. She and Becky were bound to be as horrified as I was. The truth about the Mad Max summons was more shocking than any of our fantasies.

Mum's behaviour was cruel.

It was hurtful.

It was betrayal.

Chapter 5 · Take a Chance on Me

Tania: *So what's it like when someone goes behind your back?*

Zoe: *It's unsettling. I feel very let down. I hate the thought of people talking about me — unless, of course, they're fans. And I obviously don't mind people talking about me to Luigi.*

Tania: *You mean the legendary sports shoe designer, Luigi Trellino?*

Zoe: *None other, Tania. I'm well aware what goes on, but I know most of these gossips have my best interests at heart.*

Tania: *In what way?*

Zoe: *Well, I can reveal that someone — who shall remain nameless — told Luigi I should be the first person to wear his new Sparkjet trainers. After much careful thought I agreed.*

Tania: *Ooh! Please tell us about them.*

Zoe: *All I can reveal is that they're encrusted with diamonds and rubies and are worth millions. Several pop icons and footballers were very keen to get their hands on them. But he offered them to me first.*

Tania: And on what special occasion will you show these items off to the world?

Zoe: That's a hard one, Tania. I'm hosting the MTV Europe Awards next month. That's followed by a couple of film premières and a lavish party to celebrate the birthday of a free-spending but really stupid reality TV star. When I've done all of those there's an invitation to dine at the Palace.

Tania: You mean that recently opened, trendy new nightclub in Rome?

Zoe: No. I mean The Palace – Buckingham Palace.

Tania: Astonishing!

Zoe: Yes, I was very pleased they contacted me. I've heard the catering there is pretty good.

Tania: And the Sparkjets?

Zoe: Yes, I am tempted to parade in them. However, an adviser has warned me not to take the limelight away from the female members of the royal family. Apparently they can be a bit touchy about being upstaged by other people's footwear.

'You can go in now.'

I looked up slowly and saw Mrs Perkins, the school administrator, leaning through the sliding glass hatch in her office and pointing towards Mad Max's door. She looked at me expectantly – wanting to discover the reason for my appointment. Even if I had known what Mad Max wanted, there was no way I would have told her. She was the biggest gossip to operate in a five-mile radius.

Keesha and Becky were waiting for me round the corner. They were still in shock about Mum going to Mad Max behind my back.

'I know your mum can be a bit tough, but this is out of orbit,' Becky had told me.

'Just knock a couple of times,' Mrs Perkins told me, looking disappointed that I hadn't seen fit to let her know what I was doing there.

I put my ear to his door but all I could hear was the muffled sound of a telephone conversation. I knocked twice and heard a gruff 'Enter'. I made myself focus on the task in hand, but it was hard because I was still so wound up by Mum. From the second I'd stormed out of my room last night I hadn't uttered one word to her. She'd tried to engage me in conversation several times, but I'd remained silent. I kept on asking myself, How could she do this to me? And now here I was outside Mad Max's office *because of her.*

I'd never been inside before. Sure, I'd got into trouble a couple of times (for petty things like chatting too much in class or being consistently late with handing in maths assignments – SO boring), but these incidents had all been sorted by heads of year or form tutors. His office was new territory for me. I turned the handle and walked in.

The room was a large square with a desk at the far side and an array of shelves that housed hundreds of different-coloured folders. Most of these were bulging with bits of paper. He was sitting behind the desk, looking frostily at his computer screen while talking on the phone.

'I've already tried return and nothing's happening,' he barked down the phone, 'and now I have a student with me so I'll have to go. But I expect you to sort this out later.'

He placed the receiver down and angrily gazed at his monitor for a few seconds.

I stood near the door awkwardly, not sure what to do. Without looking up, he indicated with his hand a low green chair on the other side of his desk.

I walked across the room and sat down quickly, waiting for the bombshell to explode.

He turned away from the computer and faced me.

'Zoe,' he began.

I half closed my eyes as if this action would offer me some protection from the inevitable onslaught.

'It's come to my attention that . . . '

His words hung in the air for a few seconds and I tried mentally to complete the second half of the sentence.

. . . *Your school work is abominable – your mum has asked me to give you a thirty-eight hour lecture about it.*

. . . *Your social life will be terminated for the rest of your natural life.*

. . . *Your maths assignments are so bad that you qualify for a limited time offer brain transplant.*

'. . . that you are a keen DJ.'

His words totally freaked me out. Did I hear him right? Had he spoken those six words in another language similar to English, but which in fact meant, *you are a disgrace to the whole concept of education?* And how on earth did he know about my DJing?

But I had little time to consider these questions.

'The situation is,' he continued, 'that I've agreed to the staging of a party in school on a Saturday night next month. It's going to take place in the sixth-form common room. I wasn't keen at first, but I suppose it will keep some of our pupils off the streets – at least for that evening.'

I gaped at him.

'It's obviously going to be a non-smoking, non-drinking affair, but I suppose we can't stop people dancing.'

He uttered a small laugh.

I looked at him with surprise.

Mad Max making a joke? This was getting surreal.

'In short,' he added, 'I'd like you to be in charge of the music.'

I gazed at him in shock.

'I must say that I hadn't really thought about this aspect of the evening,' he added, 'I thought they'd just play tapes. But a couple of sixth-formers said I should get a DJ and someone mentioned your name. What do you say?'

I wanted to say, *Stop being ridiculous and hand out my punishment,* but I thought that might be slightly foolish. And in that instant I had two competing phrases zapping through my head. One was THIS IS THE MOST BRILLIANT OFFER I'VE EVER RECEIVED.

And the other was WHAT IF I'M NOT GOOD ENOUGH AND END UP LOOKING LIKE A COMPLETE IDIOT?

But there could only be one answer.

'OK,' I managed to say, 'I'll do it.'

An enormous shot of relief spread over his features as if my acceptance was the most crucial deal he'd ever clinched.

'Right, that's settled then. All you need to do is tell me what sort of equipment you'll need for the night and I'll get someone on to it.'

As I sat staring at Mad Max it suddenly dawned on me that my suspicions about Mum contacting him behind my back were totally unfounded. Luckily I hadn't actually spelled it out to Mum. As far as she was concerned, I'd just been angry about her going through my books.

It must have been Keesha and Becky who'd told Mad Max about my DJing. But who approached whom? And why hadn't they just told me instead of playing along with the whole suspense thing? They could have spared me hours of worry.

'Good,' he said, suddenly turning back to his computer screen, 'we'll speak again soon. You can go now.'

I stood up and left his office in a daze. Mrs Perkins was leaning through her hatch. She was clearly desperate for some nugget of information about my meeting with Mad Max. I smiled sweetly at her, and said nothing. I strode off up the corridor and turned the corner. Becky and Keesha couldn't contain themselves.

'WELL?' they screamed at me.

I scanned their faces carefully. I didn't know whether to be angry with them or delighted.

'Thanks,' I said smiling.

Keesha looked at Becky. Becky looked at Keesha. They both looked at me.

'What do you mean?' asked Becky. 'What did your mum tell him?'

'Mum didn't tell him anything.'

'What about her looking through your books and going behind your back to him?' asked Keesha.

'It's nothing to do with Mum,' I replied. 'Someone else, or should I say some other people, talked to him.'

I looked at their puzzled faces and realised they were either the best actresses in the land or they genuinely didn't know why Mad Max had called me in.

'Wasn't it you two who spoke to him?'

'WHAT ARE YOU TALKING ABOUT?' exploded Keesha.

Their faces looked seriously puzzled. It hadn't been them. I better tell them what had happened.

'He's asked me to DJ at a school party,' I explained. 'He says someone mentioned my name. I was sure you two had told him.'

'It wasn't us who told him, but it's fantastic!' said Keesha, laughing.

'That's brilliant!' cried Becky. 'We haven't uttered a word to him. Are you sure you're not in any trouble? Are you sure you're not making this up to avoid humiliation?'

'It's true.' I grinned. 'My first gig, handed to me on a plate by Mad Max of all people.'

'Fantastic,' Keesha said, beaming. 'Congratulations.'

'Nice one!' screamed Becky.

'Hang on a minute,' I said. 'If you didn't tell him about my DJing, who did?'

They both shrugged their shoulders.

'Haven't got a clue,' said Becky.

'Me neither,' added Keesha.

It didn't take long for us to find the culprit.

We were walking in the playground five minutes later when Dan came up to us.

'Hey Zoe, how did it go with Mad Max?'

We all looked at him with surprise.

'It was you?' asked Becky.

'Of course,' said Dan with a smile. 'He was in our tutor group yesterday, banging on about some school party. He said some sixth-formers had suggested getting a DJ and I told him I knew someone.'

'WHY THE HELL DIDN'T YOU TELL ANY OF US?' shouted Becky.

'I didn't think it would come to anything, so I couldn't see the point of mentioning it.'

'We were totally freaking out!' scolded Becky.

'How do you know I'm any good?' I asked Dan, still taking this news in.

'I was at Phoebe's ninth birthday party, remember? You were spinning the tunes and it sounded great. So I thought of you when he mentioned it. Is that OK with everyone?'

I smiled with pride.

'I've got to go now,' he said, 'but I'll see you later.'

'Good for Dan,' said Keesha after he'd gone.

I leaped in the air. 'DJ Zed lands her first gig!'

'Go for it!' said Becky with a laugh.

I suddenly stopped grinning. Apart from the possibility that my DJ skills might not be quite ready for my first proper gig, there could be one tiny problem.

My mother.

I thought about it all day. What would Mum say? Dad was bound to go for it, but Mum would be so much harder to convince. She'd already made it clear where she stood on the schoolwork/DJ balance and the prospect of me doing a gig (even with Mad Max's blessing) wouldn't be welcome news for her. I'd have to do loads of extra mixing practice to be in shape for the party and she might just say no. If I was going to get the green light from her, I'd have to use all of my powers of persuasion. I composed myself on the walk home from school and prepared for battle.

'Hi Mum, how was your day?' I asked, breezily walking into the kitchen.

She looked at me suspiciously before answering.

'Fine, thank you – how was yours?'

'It was excellent. Ms Devlin was really pleased with my *Othello* essay.' (A complete lie – I hadn't even started it.)

'Good,' she replied. 'Are you still in a mood with me about looking at your books yesterday?'

'Oh that,' I said calmly, 'of course not. I was only angry for about two minutes.' (Another complete lie – I was still furious.)

The next ten minutes were spent exchanging pleasantries with her and generally being a great conversationalist – showing an interest in the French bank she was designing and laughing about the stupidity of a certain work colleague.

Dad then walked into the kitchen and I knew my moment had come.

'Mum, Dad,' I began, standing behind a chair and leaning on it, 'there's something I need to tell you.'

Their heads simultaneously swivelled in my direction as if I was controlling them with a joystick.

'Go on,' said Mum.

'I went to see Mr Maxwell today.'

Their facial expressions moved up a couple of notches on the parental worrying scale.

'Oh yes?' said Mum.

'He's asked me to DJ at a school party.'

Dad nodded thoughtfully. 'What do you reckon, Ange?'

That meant a yes from him.

Mum raised an eyebrow. She drummed her fingers on the table for a few seconds.

'I don't know,' she started. 'I've already agreed to you doing Saturdays at the radio station. I don't want you to spend all of your time preparing for this party. It could be a major distraction from your schoolwork.'

'Maybe it will make me work harder,' I countered.

'How do you figure that one out?' she asked.

'I'll stick to a really strict timetable and won't go mad practising.'

She looked at Dad and then at me. She sighed, one of those sighs that seem to take forever.

'OK, Zoe,' she said, 'you can do it, but I'll be holding you to your promise about your schoolwork.'

Yessssssssssssssssssssssssssssssssssssssssssssssssssssssssssssssssssssssss
ssssssssssss!

I ran over and hugged her.

Dad patted me on the back.

'Well done, Zoe,' he said.

I sped out of the kitchen, grinning like crazy.

And I could only think one thing.

First stop, school party.

Next stop, superstardom.

Chapter 6 • My Life as an Agony Aunt

'That one's fifteen quid,' said Rix sourly.

It was lunchtime on Friday. I'd spent most of the week in a complete haze – I kept on having to remind myself that I'd been signed up for my first gig. OK, Mad Max was the booker, but everyone's got to start somewhere.

I was in Tune Spin on a mission to buy a record bag. No DJ can dare be seen without a record bag: A) as a means of carrying records and B) as a fashion statement. And most importantly C) for their first ever proper gig. Zak had lent me twenty pounds to tide me over until I got my allowance.

'Wouldn't a handbag be better?' Rix sneered.

The guy was so amusing I doubled up with laughter. He should be a contestant on a game show for LOSERS. He was standing a metre away from me, scowling as I slowly picked up another bag and studied it intensely. He shuffled his feet and muttered to himself.

'How about that one?' I asked, pointing to a silver one with a black *Disc Power* circular logo.

'Twenty quid,' he replied.

'I'll take it,' I announced decisively.

'Are you sure about that?' he asked scornfully. 'Isn't it a bit out of your price range?'

I pulled the twenty-pound note out of my pocket and shoved it into his hand.

'Don't spend it all at once.' I grinned, slipping the bag over my head and walking out of the shop. When I glanced back, he was holding the note up to the light, shaking his head. He looked upset that it wasn't a forgery.

When I got home after school, I went up to my room and closed the door, remaining inside silently for an hour and a half. I knew that Mum would be delighted I was doing my homework. When I say 'doing my homework', what I actually mean is giving the school books on my table an occasional glance while I made the millionth and the millionth-and-first changes to my set list for the school gig. It wasn't that I had the most massive record collection and couldn't choose the best tunes. I knew which ones I was going to play – I just couldn't decide on an order.

At supper I was excellent company, as I had been every night that week. There was no way I was going to blow it. Mum was clearly impressed with the dedication I was showing to my school-work. She seemed pleased to talk to me over a leisurely meal, instead of watching me wolf down my food and then dive for the best seat in front of the TV.

Even though it was Friday night, I had no desire to go out. Keesha and Becky had asked me to some party at one of Dan's mate's houses, but I'd declined. After supper, I mixed for a couple of hours and then had a long soak in the bath. I got into bed at eleven-fifteen. Mum and Dad were already asleep and Zak had phoned to say he was staying over at a friend's house. I was just about to turn my light off, when the ring tone of my mobile sounded.

'Zoe. It's Dan.'

'Hi Dan.'

'Are you still up?' he asked.

'No, I'm sleep talking.'

'Very funny. Look, I'm a couple of streets away and I was wondering if I could pop in and pick your brains for a minute?'

'Are you with Becky and Keesha?'

'No. Keesha went home ages ago and I just walked Becky back to hers – the party was rubbish.'

'What do you want to talk about?'

'I'll tell you when I get there.'

I looked at the clock.

'OK,' I sighed.

'See you in five.'

'See you.'

I waited a few minutes, pushed my warm duvet off, grabbed a sweatshirt and pulled it over my pyjamas.

I crept downstairs and reached the door.

Dan was standing on the doorstep looking cold and unhappy.

'It's about Becky,' he said a little awkwardly.

I stifled a yawn. The last thing I wanted to do at this hour was to provide a marriage counselling session. What sort of advice could I give him, when I wasn't in a relationship myself? On the other hand, he was now friendly with Josh Stanton and, if I helped him, maybe in some way he'd repay me by telling Josh I was the most amazing chick in town. Or at least something like that.

'I just need a female perspective on some stuff,' he told me with a hopeful look.

I rubbed my tired eyelids.

'You better come in,' I said sleepily.

Chapter 7 · Movie Madness

I was worked off my feet at CHILL the next day. Everyone seemed to want photocopying done at the same time. Jade was sitting at her desk with headphones on. In front of her stood a huge tower of CDs. She was working her way through them and furiously writing notes on a large piece of paper. Some only lasted a few seconds in her CD player while others got a slightly longer listen. As I hurried around the office, I kept an eye on her, waiting for a chance to try and talk to her about Reel Love.

At two o'clock I was fighting with a jammed photocopier. There were lights flashing all over it and I was concerned that, if I didn't fix it, the damn thing would take off and start flying around the office. I'd just managed to get it working again, when I noticed Jade stretching her arms and pulling some sandwiches out of her bag. I gave her a few minutes and then glided over in her direction.

She was wiping her lips on a napkin as I approached her desk. Her frown seemed particularly deep today.

'Hi Jade,' I began, 'how's it going?'

She looked up and stared at me with irritation.

Sensing her unfriendliness, I should have walked away, but I was curious about the music mountain.

'What's with the CDs?' I asked.

I saw that the large piece of paper on her desk had a huge title – THIS WEEK'S SINGLES – and four columns: name of act, name of single, verdict, number of stars. I quickly scanned down the paper. It had ten entries, and the verdicts next to the acts and single titles were things like: Funky tune, terrible production and, Good beats, tuneless song. The number of stars she'd given ranged from two to four, with one track getting five stars.

She sighed heavily. 'I've got to sift through all of these new tunes and select a few to take to a production meeting, where we'll decide on this week's "Breakthrough Single". So, as you can see, I'm rather busy.'

'OK,' I replied, realising that now wouldn't be a good time to try and work Reel Love into the conversation. 'Can I help you in any way?'

She shook her head.

I began to walk off, but she called me back.

'Actually there is something you can do for me.'

My eyes lit up with expectation.

'Could I have a milky coffee?'

I tried hard not to let my disappointment show.

As I stood in the tiny kitchen, pouring boiling water into a mug, I analysed if I'd made any progress with Jade. Had I spotted even the tiniest of chinks in her armour? Had she warmed to me even a tiny bit? Was I any nearer to meeting Reel Love?

Despite looking at these questions from every single possible angle and applying a Keesha-like positivity in dealing with them, I knew the answer to each was pretty straightforward.

No.

'Snooty cow!' exclaimed Keesha, after I'd related my brief exchange earlier that day with Jade.

'Who the hell does she think she is?' said Becky. 'It's not like *she's* famous.'

We were waiting to buy tickets for the eight-forty-five showing of *Letting Your Hair Down* – a Canadian film about a girl whose parents want her to be a model, while she has seriously different plans for herself. Dan would have come (he normally hangs out with us on Saturday nights), but there was a football match on TV and he'd gone round to a friend's house to watch it.

The New Valley Cinema was really busy. It had only been open for a couple of weeks. It's in one of those giant retail parks, a bus ride out of town, that make you feel you're in the middle of nowhere. Once inside we were immediately dazzled by banks of TV screens suspended from the ceiling, blaring out film trailers. Everything about the place was flash and expensive. The pick 'n' mix stall was a mile long and the popcorn cost about forty pounds a kernel.

'Changing the subject for a minute,' said Keesha, 'guess who I got an e-mail from today?'

'No idea,' I replied.'

'From Tim.'

'What did that slimeball want?' Becky asked.

'You won't believe this,' Keesha said with a smile. 'He said the Australian girl turned out to be a nightmare. He's sorry for finishing with me and wants me back.'

'So what did you say?' I asked.

'I sent him a two word e-mail.'

'Saying what?' asked Becky.

'Forget it!'

'Woohoo!' yelled Becky. 'How do you feel about him now?'

'The guy's a creep. I want nothing to do with him. He's pathetic.'

I clapped my hands in support of the action she'd taken.

'Talking of special people,' said Keesha, turning to look at Becky, 'don't you have something to tell Zoe.'

'Oh yeah,' said Becky, 'I'm thinking about finishing it with Dan.'

'Why?' I asked, surprised.

'He's a lovely guy and everything, but, as we all know, he pretty much does whatever I tell him. That's nice at first, but after a while it makes you think of him as some sort of servant.'

* * *

Dan had kept me up till half past twelve the night before, spilling his heart out about Becky being the love of his life and how he was worried she would dump him. If this happened, he didn't know what he'd do. He made me promise that I wouldn't say anything to Becky about his visit.

I'd told Dan that I thought he and Becky were really suited to each other. As I doled out this reassurance, I knew that it wasn't motivated simply by wanting the best for Becky and Dan. I was also very aware that Dan's new friendship with Josh Stanton could be of crucial importance to me. I *needed* Josh (and therefore Dan) to stay in my world. If Becky finished with Dan, I'd see less of him. And, if I saw less of him, my chances to be in Josh's company would be severely diminished. Yes, it was self-centred, but it looked like my best shot of getting anywhere near my dream boy.

I also told Dan that maybe it was time for him to start sticking up for himself a bit more. Becky could be very overpowering and it would be good for him to be a bit more assertive with her. He nodded thoughtfully for a few moments after I'd said this.

'You know what, Zoe,' he said, 'I think you're right. I do tend to go with the flow, which means Becky always gets her own way.'

'Maybe you should stop bossing Dan around,' I suggested to Becky. 'See what happens if he's allowed to think for himself.'

Becky thought about this suggestion for a few seconds.

'But I like being in control.'

'That's OK,' I said, 'but Dan's great. Think of all those self-centred, arrogant boys at school who think they're God's gift to womankind. Dan's way above them.'

'I know,' said Becky.

'And he's crazy about you,' I added.

'You're right,' replied Becky. 'I know he's very into me, but he's just not . . .' she searched for the right word, 'he's not *dynamic* enough for me. At least that's what I think today. Ask me tomorrow and I'll have probably changed my mind.'

I was about to continue the Dan PR campaign, when I heard a voice calling our names across the foyer.

I spun round.

It was Gail Simmonds, advancing towards us, with Josh Stanton on her arm.

Becky and Keesha grabbed me, partly to support me and partly to stop me bolting like a horse through an open stable door.

'Hi girls,' Gail said, beaming. 'Is tonight a boy-free experience?'

Josh stood beside her, looking down at the ground. He was wearing jeans and a black-hooded top and his hair was even more spiked up at the front than usual. I so wanted to catch his eye, but I wasn't prepared to lie down on the foyer floor to accomplish this.

'It looks like it,' Becky replied coldly. 'We can have a good time with or without the male species.'

'It's slightly different for me.' Gail giggled, tugging at Josh's arm. He looked up for a second and it seemed like he was about to say something, but thought better of it.

'Enjoy your film,' said Gail with a smile, 'I don't know how much of ours we'll actually see.'

'Sounds like you'll be wasting your money then,' snorted Keesha, pulling us away from them.

'Excellent put down,' Becky said approvingly. 'Are you OK, Zoe?'

I nodded and walked with them to a bench just beyond the foyer.

Knowing Josh and Gail were an item was bad enough, having to see them together was the worst.

'Do you think he noticed me?' I asked.

Becky and Keesha looked at each other.

'Maybe he's just seeing Gail till he plucks up enough courage to ask you out,' said Keesha.

'Yeah right.'

That ranked up there with the possibility of me climbing Mount Everest in a tutu.

'Forget Josh Stanton, the ticket queue's too long,' moaned Becky. 'Let's wait for it to calm down.'

We walked around the foyer for five minutes looking at film posters and deciding which actors we'd choose to work with if we were Hollywood starlets.

'What time does the film finish?' I asked the man behind the counter when we returned to the much shorter queue.

He checked a piece of paper.

'Ten-thirty,' he replied.

'That's a pretty long film,' I said.

The man shrugged his shoulders. 'I don't make them, I just sell the tickets.'

I looked at Keesha and Becky. 'I told Mum I'd be back by eleven at the latest and there's no way I'll do it.'

'Where's your spirit?' chided Becky. 'It's Saturday night. You're fourteen, not seventy. Life's too short to worry about being a tiny bit late. And, anyway, you can call her and everything will be fine.'

The ticket guy looked at us.

'Can we have three tickets please,' Becky said, making the decision on my behalf.

Her Royal Bossiness strikes again.

He printed out our tickets and handed them over. 'The film starts in five minutes.'

We walked away from the queue and I immediately phoned home. The engaged signal beeped in my ear. Mum was working at home and she was probably locked on to the internet, trying to work out some thorny architectural problem. I tried her mobile. It was switched off.

'Typical,' I muttered.

'What's up?' asked Keesha.

'The landline's busy and she's left her mobile off.'

'What about your dad?' asked Becky.

'His mobile's broken.'

Becky put her arm round me.

'Come on, Zoe. The film's about to start and we're not having you going home by yourself because you're worried about getting home a few minutes late.'

I shook my head. 'It won't be a few minutes. It'll be more like half an hour and half an hour in Mum's world is like three hundred years in anyone else's universe.'

Becky and Keesha laughed.

'You can nip out during the film and try her again,' said Keesha. 'And anyway, even if you can't get through, we'll come in with you when you get home and tell your mum that you did your best to call her. Come on, it's not the end of the world.'

I hesitated. I'd worked my way into Mum's good books recently and I simply *couldn't* ruin that situation. My mind was screaming: *Get on a bus now and stop the forces of temptation descending on you.*

But however much I knew I should leave, the film looked good and I didn't want to rush off home like some obedient pet. And I had tried my *hardest* to call home. The girls would back me up. The circumstances were exceptional. Mum would have to understand.

'Let's do it,' I announced, 'but we leave the second the film ends.'

'Definitely,' Keesha said.

It was a great film. The heroine (who was supposed to be fifteen but was clearly in her early twenties) was determined to defy her pushy, gold-digging parents and devote her life to ethical purposes. I snuck out twice to try home but got nowhere. Landline still tied up, Mum's mobile still off.

We were out of the cinema at ten-thirty on the dot. Twenty

minutes later, a bus arrived and fifteen minutes into the journey, I got through. It was just after eleven.

Mum answered the phone immediately.

'Hi Mum, it's me.'

'Where are you?'

She sounded a tad frosty.

'I've been trying you all evening and . . .'

'Are you still with Keesha and Becky?' she asked.

'Of course. We're on the bus. Sorry, I'm a bit late – I'll be back in half an hour. Don't wait up for me.'

'Come straight home,' she commanded and hung up.

Come straight home? Where on earth did she think I was going?

The house was completely dark when we approached it. It was eleven-thirty.

'We're coming in with you,' said Keesha.

I shook my head.

'I'll be OK. I think Mum accepted my story.'

'It's the truth,' pointed out Becky.

I nodded.

'You go on. It's cool.'

We said our goodbyes and they walked off. I turned my key in the front door. The hall was silent. There was no sign of life. This was good. Mum and Dad must be asleep. I slipped my shoes off and tiptoed upstairs. Still no sign of another living being. A thin shaft of orangey-yellow light spilled from under my bedroom door.

I remembered leaving the bedside lamp on. I pushed my door open carefully.

As soon as I walked in I saw her.

Mum was standing in the middle of my room. She didn't look particularly happy.

This wasn't good.

'I tried to tell you what happened on the phone,' I blurted out. 'Keesha and Becky will back me up.'

'I don't care what Keesha and Becky say,' she snapped.

'But Mum, the landline was engaged and your mobile was switched off,' I said, trying to stay calm.

Her eyes were burning with anger. 'Yes, I was logged on for a bit and my mobile was off, but if you knew you were going to be that late, you should have come straight home.'

'So you admit it. It's not my fault I couldn't get hold of you.'

'No, I said if you couldn't get me you should have left.'

'Well why didn't you phone me if you were so worried?'

'You're fourteen, Zoe and it's about time you took on some responsibilities.'

This was very bad.

'I can't just let Keesha and Becky down because you're online. I phoned you the minute I could.'

'You know how I feel about getting-home times.'

The argument strategy clearly wasn't working so I went for the apologetic approach. 'OK, OK. Next time I'll come straight home. It won't happen again.'

'It's too late for sorry,' she said.

'What do you mean?' I asked anxiously.

'I mean exactly what I say. It's time you learned how it feels to be let down.'

'I've told you, I did my best!' I shouted.

She shook her head.

This was very bad indeed. All of my recent good work with her suddenly counted for nothing.

'I give you a lot of freedom to do what you want, but it's got to be a two-way process. I know I said you could do the gig at school, but you've blown it.'

'My being a bit late tonight has got nothing to do with the school party.'

'It has EVERYTHING to do with it. It demonstrates a complete lack of concern and responsibility.'

'PLEASE DON'T DO THIS TO ME!' I wailed.

'You're not going to the party as a DJ or as anything else.'

'That's not fair!' I yelled, tears starting to stream down my cheeks.

'It's totally fair,' she said furiously. 'I've made up my mind and that's final.'

Chapter 8 . I am a Petulant Teenager

Tania: So, Zoe, what's all this I hear about a ban being imposed on you?

Zoe: You mean the Formula One affair?

Tania: Of course. It took up hundreds of column inches in the weekend papers.

Zoe: Being banned from anything isn't particularly pleasant, but what you read was only partly true, Tania. You know how the newspapers exaggerate things.

Tania: What do you mean partly true?

Zoe: The powers that be of the motor-racing world have asked me very politely not to frequent the stands when a race is in progress.

Tania: And why is that?

Zoe: They're worried about the safety of the drivers.

Tania: How do you mean?

Zoe: Apparently, every time the drivers near the stand where I'm *sitting, they feel compelled, by a sort of magnetic force, to try and catch a glimpse of me.*

Tania: *Surely that can't be good for their concentration?*

Zoe: *Precisely. Looking sideways when you're spinning round a track at ridiculously high speeds is frowned upon by the vast majority of driving instructors. The drivers need to have eyes on the track. That means, no reading magazines in their cars and definitely no checking out beautiful women.*

Tania: *So does this mean you'll be staying away from major race meetings in future?*

Zoe: *Not at all! They've said it's OK for me to frequent the VIP bars and celebrity lounges. If a driver wants to chat to me in one of those areas, it's fine, as long as they don't bring their car.*

'It's unbelievable!' shouted Becky, a bit too loudly for the liking of the other Sunday morning customers inside Tony's. Several people turned round to look at us.

I tuned back in to the conversation.

'But you tried to phone home about a billion times,' Keesha protested.

'It's our fault,' said Becky. 'We should have come in with you.'

'It's not your fault,' I said miserably. 'It's mine. I should have gone straight home. There was no way Mum was going to be OK about it.'

'But this is your big break,' said Becky indignantly. 'It's your first chance to play for the public. Just because you got in a bit late doesn't mean she has the right to stop you doing the gig.'

'She can and she has,' I replied.

'We must be able to do something,' said Keesha.

'There is one tiny ray of hope,' I told them.

'Go on,' said Becky.

'My dad doesn't know about the ban yet. He was out all night, working on some Norwegian rock chick's debut album. He phoned Mum and said he'd be back this evening. He kept the call short so she didn't have the chance to tell him about me. When he finds out, maybe he'll try and make her change her mind.'

'You reckon he's got a chance?' asked Becky.

'It's possible,' I replied, thinking it over. 'He might say I've made a deal with Mad Max and I should stick to it. Once or twice in the past he has tamed Mum.'

Keesha played with her rings and Becky fiddled with the zip of her jacket.

They didn't look convinced.

'Do you want something to eat?' Mum asked me.

She was standing in my bedroom doorway. It was five-thirty. I'd come back from Tony's at two and had been lying on my bed since then, feeling desperately sorry for myself. After last night's drama, I'd made it perfectly clear that I wouldn't be talking to Mum in the foreseeable future, at any time or in any language. When she tried to protest in the kitchen at breakfast, I put my fingers in my ears, started singing 'la la la la la la' and ran up to my room.

'You must be hungry by now,' she said. 'Let me get you something.'

I rolled over and faced the wall, like a petulant teenager. And before I felt any guilt about such behaviour, I reminded myself that I *was* a petulant teenager. This *was* the way we're expected to behave.

Before I'd stormed out of the kitchen that morning, Mum told me that there was no way she was changing her mind, so I might as well accept the situation and just get on with my life. I mentioned the agreement with Mad Max, but she said that was my problem. I informed her that it was the cruellest blow ever struck by a parent and that I would not be 'just getting on with my life'.

She waited in my bedroom doorway for a few more seconds and then retreated. Twenty minutes later, I heard a key opening the front door. Dad was home. I heard the muffled sound of him talking to Mum and then, a few minutes later, there was a knock at my door. Dad padded across my room.

'Hi,' he began, sitting down on my bed. 'I've just done an all-night, all-day session with this crazy Norwegian woman. The music was great, but her voice is like a deranged bat.'

I rolled over to face him.

I silently prayed for maximum sympathy and some good news on the Zoe's-been-banned-from-the-most-important-event-in-world-history front.

'Mum just told me what happened last night.'

I scanned his face, trying to discover if he was on her side or mine. It was impossible to tell. Wherever he stood, I decided a sob story would be appropriate.

'This is the first time in my whole life that I've been given a chance to do something I really, really, really want to do. You must understand, Dad. My music is so important to me. It's a brilliant chance. And Mum's ruined it.'

He ruffled his hair.

Come on, Dad. Cut to the chase – hoist me out of this pit of misery.

'This is really hard for me,' he said. 'I know how much you want to do the party.'

Yes, Dad. Now bring me some glad tidings.

'But I also respect Mum's point of view.'

OK, OK. That's very diplomatic. Now forward wind to the good bit.

'And?' I asked nervously.

He shook his head.

'And you did get home later than you said you would.'

Keep cool, Zoe. He's just looking at the matter from Mum's perspective. He has to. He's married to her. It's part of the bargain. You need to pay lip-service to your partner's point of view. He's just building up to the bit when he saves the day.

'But Dad, Mum was online so the landline was engaged. And her mobile was switched off. Anyway, I was only half an hour late.'

'Well, perhaps you should have thought more carefully about the situation.'

Careful, Dad, you're starting to worry me.

'How?'

He stroked his chin.

'You could have skipped the film and come straight home. Maybe that was the sensible option. If you blow someone's trust, there's often a price to pay.'

I don't like the sound of where this is going. Please select another menu option, like: 'Help Zoe get what she wants'.

'You mean you agree with her?' I asked slowly.

He winced and looked closely at my face.

'On this occasion, yes I agree with her. I'm all for you being independent and doing your own thing, and I'll support your DJing, as long as it doesn't take over your whole life. But saying you'll be home at eleven, means being home at eleven.'

NO! This can't be Dad speaking. This person sitting on my bed is an imposter. He's a puppet operated by my mother.

'But, Dad.'

'Sorry, Zoe, that's the way it is.'

I stared in horror as my trump card fluttered swiftly out of the pack and into the dustbin.

'Please shut the door on your way out,' I said coldly, turning back to face the wall.

That evening I was sitting on my bed with Zak. He'd really tried to make Mum change her mind about the party ban, without any success. So he came in to console me and was doing a pretty good job of it.

'There'll be plenty more gigs,' he told me. 'One day you'll be fighting off all the offers.'

'Yeah right,' I said mournfully.

Just then the doorbell went.

'Leave it,' Zak said. 'It's probably for Mum or Dad.'

A few seconds later we heard footsteps on the stairs. Laura Tanner walked in.

'Hi,' Zak and I said at exactly the same time.

Laura leaned against the wall, clearly willing Zak to leave my room and go next door with her for a snog-fest. But he showed no sign of movement. He was sticking to his loyal brother role. He motioned for Laura to take a seat, which she did with a reluctant expression.

'Mum's stopped Zoe doing a gig at school and I'm just telling her that, before she knows it, she'll be a really successful DJ.'

Laura smiled at me, but didn't look particularly interested in hearing about my problems.

Zak was continuing his pep talk when the doorbell went again. We ignored it, but more footsteps sounded on the stairs. My door creaked open, and there standing in the entrance was a totally amazing looking girl, with long straight black hair, emerald eyes and awesome cheekbones.

This must be Iman, I thought.

She scanned the room.

I looked at Zak's face and realised trouble was afoot. Even though he's always seeing more than one girl, for obvious reasons, he usually likes to keep them apart. He stood up quickly, looking ever so slightly embarrassed.

'Let me do the introductions,' he said quickly. 'Laura, I'd like you to meet Iman. Iman, this is Laura.'

The penny didn't take long to drop for Laura and Iman.

'I can't believe you!' blurted out Laura. 'You two-timing creep.'

She walked over to Zak and slapped him in the face.

'Hey Laura,' he said, rubbing his stinging cheek. 'I told you I didn't want to get tied down.'

But Laura was having none of it. She was out of the door in three seconds flat.

Zak turned to Iman.

'Iman, it's great to see you. Come and sit down.'

Iman stepped forward and slapped Zak on the other cheek.

And then *she* walked out.

Zak stood in the middle of the room, nursing the two sizzling wounds on his face and looking like an embarrassed toddler who's just been discovered raiding the cookie jar.

'Good thing they don't know about Claire,' he muttered.

I put my hands over my eyes and sighed with despair, and then laughed.

'He'll see you now,' said Mrs Perkins, leaning out through her hatch. She smiled sympathetically. 'Is everything all right, dear?'

She *so* wanted to know my business – what could I have possibly done to merit two visits to the head teacher's office? It was Monday morning. What a great way to start the week.

I pushed open the door and was greeted by an almost identical sight as last time. Mad Max was sitting behind his desk, furiously typing something on to his computer keyboard.

'Good timing, Zoe. Sit down.' He nodded briskly. 'I was going to look for you at some point today to go over the details for the party.'

I looked across the desk at him, trying to work out how he was going to react to my news.

'You know the party, Mr Maxwell?' I mumbled quietly.

He nodded.

'I can't do it.'

'Excuse me?'

'I can't do the party.'

'Oh,' he said, placing the palms of his hands on the desk. He looked at me for a couple of seconds, expecting some sort of explanation.

'It's complicated,' I told him.

'I see,' he replied and for an instant I thought I actually saw a shadow of sympathy flicker over his face. But it passed immediately and I realised he was probably acting purely out of self-interest – he wanted the best DJ for the job.

'Is there someone else you could recommend?' he asked.

I shook my head miserably.

'Well, thank you for coming to see me,' he said, turning back to his computer screen. 'I'll bear you in mind if we have another party. If you're un-banned by then.'

'Yes, Mr Maxwell.'

Mrs Perkins was standing outside his office, watering a plant on a low table. I could have sworn she had the imprint of a keyhole on her left ear. She eyed me hopefully, longing for an update. I walked straight past her, smiling my sweetest smile.

Keep guessing Mrs Perkins. Keep guessing.

Keesha and Becky wanted me to go with them to Keesha's after school, but I wasn't in the mood. I needed to be alone to wallow in my despair. The same questions kept on spinning through my head: How could Mum stop me from doing the party? Why was Dad supporting her? Was this the end of happiness as I knew it?

I walked along the High Street, looking through the windows of every shop and pulling faces at the customers inside. When I turned the corner I saw two people in the middle of a barn-storming row in front of the pet store. It was Gail and Josh. A couple of caged parrots outside the shop were listening intently to their shouting. I clung to an antique shop's door front and watched with fascination. I couldn't hear what they were saying, but it looked pretty serious. I leaned back to make sure they didn't see me.

'Can I help you?' said a voice directly behind me.

A tall, stooping man with round glasses and a long thin moustache had popped his head out of the antique shop and was looking at me carefully.

'No thanks,' I replied. 'I'm just doing some human observations. I'm training to be an anthropologist.'

He eyed me suspiciously and shuffled back inside to his musty lamps and grandfather clocks. The Gail versus Josh argument was still in full flight and I crossed my fingers tightly. This might be it, I thought. This could be the moment he sees sense and dumps her. And I'll miraculously appear, lending him my shoulder to cry on. It would be perfect! He'd soon realise I was the one destined for him and lead me off towards the sunset.

But by the time I'd snapped out of this fantasy scenario, I saw that Gail and Josh were suddenly talking to each other again. Within seconds they were hugging. And then they were kissing. I groaned in despair as my daydream shattered into a thousand pieces.

'Can I interest you in a barometer?' asked a voice in the background.

I looked round.

It was the tall moustached man from the antique shop.

'Not today,' I responded miserably, 'but could you find me a new life?'

Chapter 9 • It's a Sly World

'Leave it, Zoe.' Mum was sitting at the kitchen table, staring at me. I was standing next to the fridge, as far away from her as was technically possible without knocking walls down.

I still wasn't *officially* talking to her, except for arguments.

'You've just ruined my life! Give me one good reason why I should leave it?'

'Because it's boring.'

Good point.

'I've already told you, put it down as a lesson learned,' Mum said.

I opened my mouth, displaying a giant fake yawn.

'I know you're upset,' she went on, 'but that kind of attitude won't get you anywhere, young lady. Some parents would have grounded their kids completely after something like this.'

I hate it when she calls me 'young lady'. It's like we're suddenly living in an eighteenth century novel and she's my cruel governess.

I scowled at her.

'You never wanted me to do it in the first place,' I muttered. 'I've worked really hard recently and made sure I only mixed records when I'd done all my homework, like I promised. I bet you were just waiting for me to step a tiny bit out of line to give you an excuse to ban me from the party.'

'That's rubbish, Zoe, and you know it.'

'No, it's not. You want me to be a swot at school and hope I grow out of the whole DJ thing.'

'Well, if we *must* talk about it, think sensibly for once,' she said with a sigh. 'Keeping your head above water in school might be OK for now, but it won't be any good to you when you enter the harsh grown-up world. What will happen when Keesha and Becky trot off to university and you're sleeping in some filthy squat, living off the dole and trying to make it as a DJ in some seedy club?'

'I cannot *believe* you're worried about university,' I shouted. 'That's *years* away. If you're so bothered about my future, why don't you start researching which old-age home I'll be checking into when I'm ninety.'

'Don't be rude,' she snapped. 'I don't want you to make mistakes now that you might regret in the future.'

I covered my face with my hands.

'Oh my God,' I wailed, 'you've mapped out my entire life, haven't you?'

'No. I just take a longer-term picture than you.'

'Well you can look out for my future all you want. I'm trying to sort out the mess that's called my *present*.'

'Everything OK in here?'

It was Dad poking his head round the kitchen door.

Mum shot him an exasperated look.

'Just perfect,' I muttered sulkily.

'Still talking about the school party?' he asked.

'Yes,' we both replied.

It was the first time we'd agreed about anything for days.

I saw the queue from the top of the street. It was Wednesday after school and I'd taken the Tube to town. At home, I'd finally stopped going on about the school party. I'd made my protest as loudly and strongly as possible. It had failed. I wasn't doing it. 'Determined Dot' had to accept defeat occasionally. There was no way I'd ever forgive Mum (and Dad), but I wasn't going to run away from home. I liked central heating and Dad's cooking too much. And Zak was great to live with. If I had to carry on living in the same house, I might as well make it as bearable as possible. Plus, if anything else decent came up I'd still need Mum and Dad's agreement. If I continued being a complete misery, they'd automatically say no to anything.

I'd left them a note in VERY BIG LETTERS, stating: A) WHERE I WAS GOING, B) HOW I WAS GETTING THERE, C) WHAT TIME I'D BE HOME.

The police had put up railings along the front of the massive Sly Records Store on Tottenham Court Road. There were five policemen and several Sly Records security guards standing outside the store's entrance. I cursed myself for chatting outside school with Keesha and Becky. It had given everyone else a thirty-minute advantage over me. Also, the Tube to town seemed to take forever. I knew it was going to be busy, but this looked mad.

It had been trailed on CHILL last night – Reel Love would be at Sly Records between five and six, doing a short live set and then signing copies of his new single. Not content with re-mixing other people's stuff, he also wrote and produced his own music. I hurried to the back of the queue. There must have been about three hundred people in front of me and that was only in the street. God knows how many there were inside. Most of the crowd were my age or a bit older. There were a couple of women who looked Mum's age. Maybe they were music freaks. Or perhaps they just went for younger men.

At ten past five, there was suddenly screaming inside the store and a minute later I heard the loud thud of bass and drums. The screaming died down. Several people near me started pushing in an attempt to get nearer the entrance. But this only resulted in them being pushed back. The queue showed no signs of movement.

I stood around for a few more minutes, listening to the beat pulsating inside the store, and then 'Determined Dot' suddenly took over. I edged my way back out of the queue and walked along the railings towards a Sly Records security guard. He looked very serious. And very big. And very unfriendly.

'Hi,' I shouted above the music.

He looked down at me silently.

'My name's Zoe Wynch and I work at CHILL FM. Is there a VIP entrance?'

'Where's your ID?' he asked gruffly.

I didn't have any, but I still rummaged around in my jacket pocket for a couple of seconds.

'I must have left it at the station.'

He stared at me as if viewing a small and repulsive species of insect.

'No ID, no entry,' he stated.

I desperately thought about my next line.

'I'm actually helping to run the event. It might fall apart if I'm not in there.'

A smile flickered across his lips.

'And I'm the Prime Minister,' he replied, smirking.

I was desperately searching for a more convincing argument when I saw Jade Bell. She was hovering around the store entrance, wearing an ID tag round her neck. She knew who I was now. She knew I was mad about Reel Love. Maybe she could get me in. As I stepped away from the guard, Jade turned her head and looked directly at me. I waved and started moving quickly towards her. But I was only halfway when she turned away and disappeared inside the store. I was about to shout her name when a policeman blocked my path.

'Sorry. There's no entry this way. You'll have to go to the back of the queue like everyone else.'

Jade had seen me. She could easily have got me in, but she'd just looked straight through me. I stood on tiptoes, straining to catch a glimpse of her or Reel Love, but all I could see was a huge mass of people in the store. The decks must be round the corner by the twelve-inch records. I recognised the track he was playing. This event was designed specifically for me. I was a DJ. How many other people in the crowd could say that about themselves? My rightful place was inside.

I stamped my foot with frustration and thought about telling the policeman my life story. But what was the point? There was no way he'd buy it. And I didn't want to make a run for it and risk being arrested. If Mum was furious when I got home half an hour late from the cinema, how mad would she be if she had to collect me from a police station?

I walked back along the railings, looking at the ever-increasing queue. It did cross my mind to join their ranks again, but it could be hours before I got inside. I walked forlornly past the end of the queue and headed for the Tube.

'She completely blanked me!'

Keesha and Becky were sitting on my bed listening to my rant. I'd called them from the tube station and told them to meet me at home.

'I see her every Saturday at CHILL,' I continued, 'and she turned away. Can you believe it?'

Keesha smiled sympathetically.

'Cruel,' she said. 'Some people are so unkind.'

'Yeah,' agreed Becky. 'Unbelievable.'

Keesha quickly changed the subject.

'We really need to talk about Becky and Dan.'

'What about them?' I asked, irritated that the topic of conversation had switched even though I'd only just started on my tale of injustice. Surely Jade Bell ignoring me was a more pressing topic of conversation than Becky and Dan? We talked about their relationship all the time.

'I listened to you, Zoe. I've decided not to dump him,' said Becky. 'I'm just going to tell him to stand up to me when I'm being too overbearing.'

'Nice one.' I said. 'Anyway what do you reckon about Jade?'

'Let's talk about that later,' said Keesha. 'First we need to sort Becky out.'

'I think this calls for a session at Tony's,' added Becky. 'Just for an hour.'

'I'll give it a rain check,' I muttered, feeling aggrieved that my Jade story had been relegated to Any Other Business.

'Come on, Zoe, it'll be a laugh,' said Keesha.

'No thanks,' I replied sulkily. 'I'm not in the mood for laughs. I want to talk about Jade.'

'We will,' replied Keesha, 'but Becky and Dan are a priority.'

'And me being treated like a bag of dirt isn't?'

I was really wound up.

'Don't be so sensitive,' said Becky. 'I just need to talk about my relationship. Come on, let's go to Tony's.'

I shook my head angrily. 'I need to get in some mixing.'

Becky looked across at Keesha.

'Forget about mixing for once,' said Becky. 'You can't spend your whole life locked up in your bedroom with only records for company. It's unhealthy. Hang out with the humans.'

'It's not unhealthy,' I snapped, 'and anyway I don't spend my whole life locked up in here. I was out this afternoon at Sly Records being ignored by Jade Bell, if you need reminding.'

'You're not even doing the school gig,' Becky said. 'So you don't need to practise for anything specific.'

This comment prodded me further towards rage.

'I don't care about not doing the school gig,' I spluttered angrily. 'If you're not interested in hearing about Jade Bell, then you're not interested in me or anything that matters to me. And if I'm ever going to make it as a DJ, I need to practise. Surely you realise that by now.'

'You'll have plenty of chance to practise,' said Keesha. 'Just relax. Don't waste your energy.'

My temper was spiralling out of control. On this occasion there was no way I was going to let Becky boss me around, or Keesha smother me with the 'power' of positive thinking.

'You'll be fine without me,' I snarled.

They looked at me with bewilderment.

'Don't be like that,' said Becky. 'We're your best mates. Just forget about DJing for an hour. Don't put music before us.'

'I'm not putting music before anyone,' I shouted. 'I just wanted to talk about this afternoon. And I don't want to go to Tony's.'

'Fine, be like that!' said Keesha.

'Fine!' I said angrily. 'Just go. Go on. Get out!'

I hadn't meant to say this. It just sort of popped out. They both looked really shocked.

'OK,' said Becky, 'we're out of here.'

They stood up together and marched out of my bedroom.

In my three years at Cahill there had only been a few occasions when we'd had words with each other and only ever over trivial things. This was altogether more serious. I heard the front door open and close and looked out of my window. Keesha and Becky were walking up the street. Neither of them looked back.

I marched across my room in fury. Who needs mates like that? I asked myself. They wouldn't even listen to a simple story. If they won't support me they can go to hell!

But half an hour later I wasn't so full of bravado.

If Josh Stanton getting together with Gail Simmonds wasn't bad enough.

And Mum banning me from doing the school gig hadn't added to my woes.

Then this was far worse.

I'd just gone and completely blown it with my best mates.

Chapter 20 . Frozen Cut

During morning break I was moping about outside the hall. There was lots of activity inside. People were putting up tables and carrying cases and files.

'What's happening in there?' I asked a tall boy who was struggling beneath the weight of three boxes.

'Sixth-form university fair,' he muttered grumpily. 'It's just my bad luck that I was passing Mad Max's office when he was looking for someone to help.'

He walked on and I followed him into the hall. Lots of universities had stands and people were putting up posters, building display boards and laying out information sheets. I picked up a couple of glossy brochures and flicked through them. They all featured colour photographs of white-toothed, smiling students, sitting on large areas of grass, chatting and smiling. A couple of them were looking at books.

I suddenly remembered what Mum had said to me about

Keesha and Becky going to uni and me being left behind, struggling to make it as a DJ. I hated to admit it, even if it was only to myself, but maybe she was on to something. There were thousands of other people out there who wanted to be DJs. What if I simply wasn't good enough? What if I couldn't make a living as a DJ?

Maybe I needed to accept that there was absolutely no certainty I'd progress up the DJ ladder. Maybe I needed a Plan B. What if I was letting my schoolwork suffer at the expense of mixing and I was seriously cutting down my options?

Stop it, I commanded myself, you're buying into Mum's anti-DJ campaign. Surely you can do music, study and have a social life?

But however much I tried to convince myself that everything was going to be OK, I left the hall feeling distinctly unsettled.

I hadn't said anything about my falling-out with Keesha and Becky to Mum and Dad, but I told Zak. He was brilliant about it and reassured me that we'd be mates again in the very near future. It was kind of him to try and cheer me up, but I didn't buy it. Keesha and Becky were steering totally clear of me. For the whole week after our bust-up, they sat well away in lessons and disappeared at break times. I was still furious with them and they were obviously still angry with me, which was understandable. I *had* thrown them out of my house, and maybe that was a bit over the top. I'd only done it because they hadn't listened to me though. It felt like they didn't care about me, and I was determined not to apologise to them.

But I did desperately miss them. I floundered about like someone who's just landed in the fourth dimension and can't quite work out how to get home before the Zurgons eat them. My safety mat had been tugged away from beneath me and I was free-falling.

A week later and we still hadn't made up. The Saturday of the school party arrived. I was forbidden from attending the event and, even if I had been allowed to go, I'd have had no one to go with. If it hadn't been for my stint at CHILL FM, I'm sure I would have spent the whole day moping in bed.

For once things were pretty quiet at the station. I'd made all of the coffees and done everyone's photocopying by one o'clock. Jade was nowhere to be seen. There wouldn't be any point talking to her anyway. I was the invisible girl as far as she was concerned. There was another enormous pile of CDs on her desk. I sidled across the room and saw a large, blank piece of paper beside them. I was about to walk away when a thought suddenly hit me. I quickly scanned the room. People were hunched over computer terminals or talking on the phone. I bit my bottom lip for a minute and then slowly eased myself into Jade's chair, pulling over a CD player that was propped against a small stack of books. There were about thirty CD singles in the pile. I pulled off the first one. 'Beat Back' by Two Crew featuring The Love Dish. I quickly checked the drawers of Jade's desk and found some headphones. I slipped them on, put the CD into the machine and pressed play.

Two Crew seemed to be OK, but The Love Dish was awful.

He couldn't sing or rap. I wrote THIS WEEK'S SINGLES on a piece of paper and drew four columns: name of act; name of single; verdict; number of stars. My verdict was: Tune OK, vocals rubbish. I gave it one star. I looked around. Surely someone must have seen me and was about to swoop down on me. But everyone else in the room was far too busy to notice my actions. I grabbed the second CD: Dinah Johns – 'Found in You'. I stuck it on. It had a slow groove and when the vocals came in, I sat up in the chair. Dinah had a great voice. I picked up the pen: Excellent, slow tempo, great soulful voice. I gave Dinah four stars.

By the time I was on the third track, I was totally oblivious to the world around me. Ninety minutes later, I was just writing a comment for the twenty-sixth track, when I sensed a presence at my side. I looked up. It was Jade. She was staring at me intently as if to say, 'HOW DARE YOU SIT AT MY DESK, YOU FOUL CREATURE?'

I hurriedly pulled off the headphones and waited for the onslaught.

'What's going on?' she asked, looking at the pile of CDs and my two pages of notes.

'I'm really sorry. I saw you weren't here and I thought I could help you out. So I started listening to the tracks and making notes. I saw you doing it last week. I know I should have asked you.'

She eyed me coldly and took the headphones. She scanned my pieces of paper and picked up the Two Crew featuring The Love Dish CD. She put it in the CD player and listened on the headphones. Her expression remained unchanged. She listened for about forty-five seconds and then took out the disc and replaced it with the Dinah Jones track. There was still no emotion on her face. She listened for a minute and then pulled the headphones off and picked up my first sheet of paper.

I sat in her chair trying to work out what her exact words would be.

Never come within five miles of me again.

I'll be recommending several years in solitary confinement.

I will make sure that you NEVER, EVER get a chance to become a DJ even on hospital radio.

But then something remarkable happened.

She smiled.

It wasn't a complete smile because that would have been too weird. But it was definitely an 'absence of frown'.

'You're right,' she said. 'The vocals on the Two Crew tune are rubbish.'

I breathed a massive sigh of relief.

'And Dinah Jones sounds promising. I might have even given her five stars. But four is probably right.'

Was I hallucinating?

'You seem to have a good ear for a decent track,' she said. 'What sort of stuff do you normally listen to?'

At last! A chance to talk about music in a music radio station!

'You know I'm a massive Reel Love fan. I've got all of his singles and most of the re-mixes he does. I'm also into rare Seventies dance tunes, a bit of hip-hop and some soul tracks.'

She looked impressed.

Despite all previous evidence to the contrary, it looked like Jade might be human.

'And I really want to be a DJ,' I added.

She was silent for a few seconds.

'It's a tough game to break into,' she eventually said, 'especially as a female. There are quite a few men out there who are still living in the dark ages – they think that real DJs can only be blokes. It's pathetic really.'

An image of Rix flickered through my mind. 'I know the kind of people you're talking about,' I replied.

She studied the piece of paper in her hand for another minute.

'This is good work,' she said. 'To tell you the truth, I find it a real chore to go through these every week. After a while they all merge into one unending track.'

The woman, who'd previously completely ignored me and blanked me outside Sly Records, was PRAISING me!

And she wasn't finished.

'Why don't you carry on and finish the last few? If that's OK with you?'

If that's OK with me! I would listen to a thousand CD singles if she wanted me to.

'Sure,' I said with delight.

She started walking off, but after a few steps she turned back to me.

'Would you like a coffee, Zoe?'

I stared at her with disbelief.

'Yes,' I managed to reply, 'milk and one sugar please.'

I was still on a high as I walked home later that afternoon. When I'd finished with the CDs, Jade looked over all of my work and nodded approvingly. She told me she'd be taking the six singles I'd given four or five stars, to a production meeting. It was then up to the production team to choose that week's CHILL 'Breakthrough Single'. It was all so strange. I expected Jade to laugh at me any minute and say she was just pretending to be pleased, but as the day wore on I had to accept that she was being genuine. She even told one of the station managers about my initiative. For the first time I felt part of the set-up at CHILL and not just like a deranged odd-job girl.

But my feeling of joy didn't last too long because I soon remembered the school party that night. I sat in the sitting room looking half-heartedly through old copies of *In the Mix* trying not to think about the gig. I fetched some cereal from the kitchen and took it up to my bedroom. I flicked through several TV channels. I tried to work out if I was the hardest-done-by teenager on the Earth's surface.

I took a vote and decided I was.

As it started to get dark I thought about Keesha and Becky getting ready for the party. There would be a major fashion show in Becky's bedroom with loads of 'try-outs'. Then they'd finally decide which outfit was the one and they'd spend ages doing their hair and make-up. I thought for a few seconds about donning a disguise and sneaking out of the house. But knowing Mum, she'd have security service agents stationed at every street corner, looking out for me.

At about eight o'clock Zak came into my room. He was wearing jeans, a collarless black shirt and trainers. He was going to the school party with some of his mates from Sixth Form college.

'I'm heading off,' he said guiltily. 'I just came to say goodbye.'

'Bye,' I said quietly.

'Sorry you're missing it,' he said. 'I bet it's rubbish.'

'It's not the end of the world.'

He put his arm round my shoulders.

'That's the spirit,' he said.

'Actually,' I said, 'it is the end of the world, but I'll get over it.'

He squeezed my arm sympathetically and left.

The party started at eight-thirty and, as this time came and went, I began to think about all the party-goers having an amazing time. I tried to imagine what they'd all be wearing and what the sixth-form common room would look like. And who had Mad Max got to take my place? What sort of tunes were they playing? Would everyone be dancing?

At nine, I got up off my bed and pulled my headphones on. I flipped a couple of records on to my decks and cranked the volume up. Even though I'd been forcing myself to be pleasant to my parents, this was the night they'd destroyed for me. Maybe some loud music would remind them of the crime they'd committed. It was about twenty minutes before Mum came up and complained about the noise. When she appeared in my bedroom doorway, I shrugged my shoulders. I couldn't hear what she was saying.

Eventually I did turn it down, but carried on mixing while constantly checking the time. I felt like my bedroom clock was taunting me, and a couple of times I could have sworn its hands started going backwards. At eleven I lay down on my bed and studied my bedroom ceiling. Midnight arrived and soon after I heard Zak's key in the door. Thirty seconds later, he came into my room.

'Are you still awake?' he whispered, looking at me sprawled out on my bed.

'I've never been more awake,' I answered miserably.

'How are you doing?'

I ignored this question.

'Was it good?' I asked.

'It was OK,' he said shiftily.

I took his response as a sign that it was the greatest party ever.

'Who did the music?' I asked.

'I don't know his name,' Zak answered, sitting beside me. 'Some guy who works at that record place you go to on the High Street.'

Rix!

'Not a guy with a goatee?' I groaned.

Zak nodded. 'Someone said his dad knows one of the school governors and the news reached Mad Max.'

I jumped off my bed and started pacing up and down my room.

'Was he any good?' I asked nervously, praying that Zak would say he was several rungs below complete garbage.

Zak looked at the floor for a second.

'He was fine,' Zak replied.

'How fine?' I demanded.

Zak thought about this for a few seconds.

'As far as DJs go, he seemed to know what he was doing. No major screw-ups. But I'm sure you'd have done better.'

My brother was trying to protect me from the truth. Rix had been stunning. He'd earned himself a place in the league of master mixers. While I'd been clock watching at home, he'd been revelling in the crowd's adoration. If Mad Max ever allowed another school party to go ahead, he wouldn't come knocking on my door. I was the pathetic little kid whose mum forbade her from going to the party. Wonder Boy Rix would be sure to get the call.

I was still preoccupied with Keesha and Becky on the Monday after the gig. I'd spent the whole of Sunday imagining what a top time they would have had the night before. I went into the toilets before my first lesson and saw them standing and laughing in front of the mirror. They were talking about the party in loud voices. The minute I walked in they went completely silent. I opened my mouth to say something, but changed my mind, spun on my heels and walked out. I still wasn't prepared to make the first move.

During lunch break, I sped to Tune Spin. I hoped that Rix had no idea I was the person he'd replaced for the school party. And if he did know, I *prayed* that he didn't know I'd been *banned* from doing it by my mum. That would give him verbal ammunition for several years.

Luckily when I stepped inside, Rix was nowhere to be seen. There were a couple of earnest-looking guys in their early twenties, checking out some racks on the far side. I started rifling through the hip-hop section. There were some new tunes I'd never heard. I glanced across at the decks. Rix was still out of sight. I grabbed four records and hurried across the floor, in case my courage left me. It was time for decisiveness. It was time for mixing.

I put the headphones on and placed a record down. I pulled up the fader and the tune started pumping out of the speakers. It sounded good. I gave myself a mental pat on the back. *I was doing it.* I picked up another record, slipped it on to the second deck and started lining it up.

It was then that Rix appeared at the counter. He looked in my direction with shock. He folded his arms and stared. *He didn't like it.* Here was some lowly schoolgirl treading on his turf. I could tell by his expression that he was aching for me to mess up. I gave the first track another minute and then slowly started fading in the second. The beats were totally in synch. I increased the volume of the second track but let the first one play for another thirty seconds, before fading it out. I have to say it sounded OK. I looked up and saw Rix still standing there, watching me with contempt. He slowly hand-clapped after the mix.

You're pathetic, my mind screamed at him but I knew I had to ignore him. And I suddenly felt a surge of pride welling inside me.

I'd completed my first mix in Tune Spin, and I'd done all right. There was no way I was going to step down now. I spun another record on to the slipmat and sped it up.

Ten minutes later, I'd done a couple more mixes and they'd all been pretty good. I felt warm with satisfaction and walked over to the counter. Rix was busy untangling some speaker cable. I coughed loudly.

He slowly put his pen down and looked up at me.

'What do you want?' he scowled.

'I was wondering if you could get hold of these two,' I said, handing over the latest copy of *In the Mix*. Two American tracks were circled in green ink. He looked at the magazine for a couple of seconds as if I'd just dropped a used handkerchief into his palms.

'Dunno,' he muttered.

'Well,' I said slowly as if talking to a two-year-old, 'you either can order them or you can't.'

He eyed me with contempt. 'Yeah, I can order them if I want to.'

'Well I want you to order them.'

He started cursing and muttering as he roughly pulled out a piece of paper from a box file.

'Fill this out,' he said, pushing the tatty photocopied order form over the counter. 'They're imports so they may take ages to get here.'

'Have you got a pen?' I asked.

He scrabbled around on the counter and handed me a chewed blue biro.

'How long is ages?' I enquired, as I filled out the form.

'Could be a couple of weeks. Could be months.'

'Which is more likely?'

He shrugged his shoulders. 'No idea.'

'Fine,' I said, handing him back the completed form.

'You need to leave a deposit.'

'How much?' I asked.

'A tenner.'

I only had seven pounds in my purse.

'I haven't got ten,' I said. 'How about a fiver?'

A smirk spread across his face. The guy looked positively delighted. He wasn't going to waste this opportunity to indulge in some Zoe-baiting.

'Sorry, but you have to leave ten,' he repeated with obvious glee. 'It's shop policy. I don't know what happens in fashion boutiques, but that's the way it works here.'

'Come on, I've seen you bend that rule for loads of people,' I protested.

He pondered this proposition for a few seconds, enjoying the moment.

'All right,' he said reluctantly, 'just this once.'

I handed over the money.

He scribbled, 'Deposit – five pounds' on the order form and clipped it into a ring-binder file.

'Thank you,' I said as politely as I could.

But the guy couldn't resist having another dig.

'Maybe one day you'll earn your own money,' he sneered.

I stared at this living model of immaturity. Don't rise to the bait, girl, I commanded myself.

So, I walked across the floor in the most dignified way possible. Unfortunately I didn't look where I was going and, as I stepped outside, I walked straight into someone standing there. My school bag flew off my shoulder and I fell over on the pavement along with the person I'd bumped into. I angrily turned my gaze on whomever it was I'd collided with and prepared to scream at them for being so clumsy.

But no words came.

My mouth hung open like an oval entrance to a rocky cave.

I knew my collision partner.

It was Josh Stanton.

The contents of my bag were strewn all over the ground. Josh pulled himself up. I looked at him. He was eyeing me with concern. His eyes looked even better from up close. He offered me his hand.

Josh Stanton offered me his hand. The age of chivalry wasn't yet dead.

I grabbed my school bag off the floor and reached out for his hand. For approximately five seconds, I was holding Josh Stanton's hand. Surely that meant something. Somewhere.

Our hands separated and he kneeled down to pick my things up off the floor. Thank God there weren't any embarrassing items in there – a couple of English textbooks, my mobile and some lip-gloss. He handed them over to me and I stuffed them back inside my bag. I tried to look as cool as possible. Which is hard when you're flustered, embarrassed and have strawberry-coloured cheeks.

'Are you all right?' he asked.

This is your big conversation chance, Zoe. Your choice of words could change your life forever.

'S'OK,' I mumbled.

S'OK?

That is not a word.

S'OK!

Don't look it up in a dictionary, Zoe. It's nonsense.

Talk to him, you idiot!

But I was terrified of saying something else ridiculous.

Speak! Form some words!

But my mouth remained firmly closed. I couldn't even manage a 'Thank you'. I just smiled goofily at him. He smiled back and then spoke to me again.

'I should look where I'm going in future.'

I carried on gazing at him for a few more seconds and then realised I needed to do something. So I did what came naturally. I started walking away up the High Street, cursing myself for missing a golden opportunity. I so badly wanted to look back, but I forced myself not to.

Zoe Wynch – graceful seductress? Or clumsy peanut-brain?

Chapter 22 · Gig Alert

Tania: So Zoe, I hear you've been bumping into some fascinating characters recently.

Zoe: Yes, Tania. It's been very strange. They just seem to turn up wherever I go.

Tania: The press mentioned Matt Nash from boy band Got-a-go.

Zoe: For once the papers are right about something. I was shopping in town for yachts and this guy appears at my side in a store guard's outfit. When he started talking I realised who it was. I've been crazy about him for ages.

Tania: What did you say?

Zoe: I was about to launch into a lengthy conversation when one of the real store guards approached us and threw him out.

Tania: And wasn't there a story about the singer, Darren Byecroft?

Zoe: Yeah, later that day, I'd just left a jewellery shop, when I noticed someone on a skateboard tailing me. When I went to confront him, he parked the board and took off his helmet. I was completely stunned to see Darren. He said he'd nearly lost me several times because the skateboard didn't go very fast inside shops.

Tania: And then what happened?

Zoe: A traffic warden appeared from nowhere and gave Darren a parking ticket. His board was parked on a double yellow line. Darren was furious and as they started arguing I slipped away.

Tania: And Miles Forge, the leading record producer?

Zoe: I found him camping outside my house one morning. He had a small tent and some provisions.

Tania: Incredible!

Zoe: Weird I call it. I said I wasn't a camping person. I prefer five-star hotels.

Tania: How did he respond to that?

Zoe: He was massively disappointed. I jumped on a bus and last thing I saw of him, he was trying to pull the tent down but had got tangled up in the ropes.

'She's calling you,' hissed a couple of boys walking in front of me.

I was in the corridor after one of Mad Max's legendary assembly outbursts. The source of his anger this time had been obscene graffiti in the toilets. He couldn't quite bring himself to share the words he'd chanced upon, but he got so worked up that I genuinely thought he might internally combust. He warned us that he'd find the culprits and then happily hand them over to the police. When he uttered this threat, a few people shuffled uncomfortably in their seats and several school bags containing aerosol canisters were zipped tightly closed.

I looked round and saw Ms Devlin beckoning me towards her.

'Zoe, can I have a word?' she asked.

If it was about my concentration span in her lessons, I could do without it. My life was already complicated enough. I followed her into the seating area near Mrs Perkins's room and Mad Max's office. Mrs Perkins was at her hatch. She eyed me with curiosity, but I stared her out and she shifted her gaze.

'What's going on?' Ms Devlin asked, watching me with her big, concerned, teacher eyes as we sat down on two low armchairs.

I looked blankly at her.

'How d'you mean?' I asked.

'I'm not stupid, Zoe. I can see you've fallen out with Keesha and Becky. You three are usually the tightest group. You've been sitting well away from them in class. Do you want to talk about it?'

I sighed heavily and decided not to tell her what was on my mind. Spilling your heart out to a teacher is always more trouble than it's worth.

A minute later I was telling her what was on my mind and spilling my heart out. Some teachers are really good at getting you to talk to them. Maybe they learn a form of hypnosis at teacher-training college. I told her about my DJing, the row with Keesha and Becky, being banned from doing the gig, Mum giving me a hard time about my schoolwork and my worries about the future.

The only thing I left out was Josh Stanton. There was no *way* I was going to talk to Ms Devlin about him. I still possessed a tiny crumb of dignity even after sending him flying after our recent collision.

Ms Devlin smiled whimsically when I'd finished telling her about my fall-out with Keesha and Becky.

'I can totally relate to what you're saying,' she said. 'I was constantly arguing with my friends at school. Maybe it's a girl thing. Boys tend to punch the daylights out of each other, make some primal sounds and then everything's fine again. But girls are more subtle. They fight *psychological* wars.'

I sat for a minute thinking about this.

'Should I just forget about them and find some new mates?' I asked, half-joking.

She shook her head.

'No, of course not. They're really good friends. It just needs one side to break the ice. There's probably truth in both of your arguments. You felt they weren't listening to you. They think you're too obsessed with your music. I'm sure you'll find a way to compromise. You need to accept that they're not as gripped by DJing as you are. They need to give you the chance to talk about music sometimes but not all of the time.'

'I knew you were going to say something like that,' I said.

'It will work out with Keesha and Becky.'

'What about my mum?'

'Mother-daughter relationships can be quite intense,' she replied. 'Whenever I go home to see my mum, she still treats me like a three-year-old.'

'But I reckon Mum wants me to give up DJing completely and turn into some sort of no-life geek,' I whimpered.

'Do you know that for a fact?' she asked.

'She makes it pretty obvious.'

'She only wants the best for you.'

I sighed. 'That's what she's always telling me, but it doesn't feel like that.'

'When did you ever hear a teenager and their mum agreeing about anything serious?'

'Never,' I replied.

'Exactly.' She nodded. 'The best thing you can do is try and get your DJ/schoolwork balance right. Then she won't be able to criticise you so easily.'

'But I thought I was doing that.'

'OK, but she clearly doesn't see it that way. Maybe you need to tell her exactly how you're going to achieve that balance. Perhaps you need to say something like, tonight I'm going to do two hours homework and then an hour's mixing. Spell it out for her in detail.'

I pulled a face at her. Did she really expect me to keep Mum informed of my minute-by-minute activities?

'Give it a try, Zoe. It's amazing what a little information can do to build bridges.'

'What about my doomed future?' I asked. 'You know, me as a drop-out and my friends as star university students?'

She smiled wryly.

'First off,' she replied, 'university is years away. And secondly you can go to university and pursue your interest in DJing.'

'Mum thinks university is for academic stuff. She often talks about how hard *she* studied.'

Ms Devlin clasped her hands together.

'Come on, Zoe. The world's a very different place since your mum went to university. She's probably a bit out of touch with what courses are on offer.'

'Knowing my mum,' I said, grimacing, 'she's probably visited every university in the country and decided where I'll be going.'

'Come on,' said Ms Devlin, grinning, 'she can't be that bad.'

I looked at her with a pained expression on my face.

'She's worse,' I muttered.

'I'm sure she's not, Zoe. All mums worry about their kids. It's what they do. It's in the instruction manual.'

I nodded thoughtfully. 'What about Keesha and Becky? Should I say sorry?'

'That's totally up to you. If you don't want to, that's fine. But if you want to heal things quicker, then yes, go to them. Swallow your pride and make things up.'

'Thanks for the chat,' I said, standing up.

She laughed. 'Teachers aren't just interested in whiteboards and textbooks.'

At that second Mad Max appeared.

'Can I have a word Ms Devlin?'

I picked up my stuff.

Ms Devlin gave me a thumbs-up and then stood up to talk to Mad Max.

I was on my way home, when I heard my name being called.

'Zoe, wait up!'

It was Dan sprinting up the High Street after me. He stopped when he reached me and said he needed to talk. My heart sank. I was in no mood to offer him more relationship counselling about Becky. I wasn't even talking to the girl. We sat down on a bench outside the library.

'Thanks for listening to my moaning that night,' he said. 'You made me feel much better about it.'

'No worries,' I replied, waiting for episode two of my career as an agony aunt.

'You, Becky and Keesha have had a bit of a bust-up, haven't you?'

'It's no big deal,' I lied.

'Of course it's a big deal. You three are like sisters. Whatever you've argued about, it can't be so bad that it ruins your friendship.'

I shrugged my shoulders.

'Is that why you wanted to talk to me?' I asked.

He shook his head.

'Go on.'

'You know my brother Howie fancies himself as a bit of a promoter?'

I nodded.

'He's putting on a night at the Gate Sports Centre in Tufnell Park. It's going to be a fourteen to seventeen's party. You know the kind of thing.'

'Sounds good,' I said, not really concentrating on what he was saying.

'The thing is,' explained Dan, 'the guy who was going to DJ for Howie broke his arm yesterday and has pulled out of the gig. Howie needs to find a replacement quickly.'

My ear antennae suddenly snapped into place. I felt a spark of excitement flutter in my chest.

'I've put your name forward to Howie. He wants to hear what you can do.'

First Dan puts in a word for me to Mad Max and now he's selling my talents to his brother. Was this guy my agent or what?

I raised both of my fists in the air.

'DJ Zed rides again,' I shouted.

'I'm sure he'll go for you,' Dan said, grinning. 'It's in a couple of weeks so you've got plenty of time to get your act together . . . Listen, I've got to go, I'm late for football practice but let me know when we can come over and listen to your stuff.'

I wanted to ask if Josh was going to be at the practice, but Dan was clearly in a bit of a hurry. He ran off back down the High Street and I watched him till he was out of sight. I felt a surge of satisfaction at the small part I'd played in encouraging Becky to stay with him. He was a good guy and, if he could just challenge her bossiness when it became too overwhelming, then maybe they had a future – I thought they were good together. And he was right about Becky and Keesha. We were like sisters. But I still wasn't convinced that I should be the one to thaw my icy relations with them.

I was fired up by the prospect of the sports centre gig, but my excitement was laced with a pretty huge problem going by the name of Angela Wynch. I was sure Dad would be cool about the gig, but what would Mum say? Surely I'd paid my penalty for the cinema fiasco? I'd been punished and I'd suffered. But would she let me do this one (if Howie thought I was any good), or had she taken such a rigid stance against DJing that any gigs were out of the question? This possibility was too horrendous to contemplate.

I picked up my bag and carried on walking home deep in thought. And then that age-old question floated into my head. What would happen if Mum did agree to me doing it but I wasn't up to scratch? I *had* put in hours and hours of practice, but playing in your bedroom doesn't compare to doing a set in front of hundreds of people. But I knew that if I didn't do my first real set soon, I'd still be doing private bedroom gigs when I was fifty.

I opened the front door and heard Mum talking loudly on the phone in her study. What would I tell her when Dan and Howie came to listen to my mixing?

Should I be truthful about Howie's party?

Or should I tell a gigantic lie?

Chapter 12. SOFA so Good

On the Saturday following the school party, I was sitting at CHILL, filing away meeting notes and thinking about what I was going to do that night. My options were limited. I was still living on a different planet from Keesha and Becky – our fall-out seemed to have gone on forever. And I wasn't prepared to go trawling through the social b-list in my diary.

I was also really nervous about Dan and Howie's visit the next morning. I kept going over in my head the mini-set I'd prepared for them. I was just about to put another packet of paper in the photocopier when I sensed someone standing next to me.

'Zoe, are you up for doing the singles trawl again?'

Jade was there holding a great stack of CDs.

I was still very wary of her but saw at once she was serious.

'Definitely,' I replied.

'Use my desk,' she added.

She passed over the discs and I tottered across the room,

placing them carefully down. I plucked out a fresh piece of paper and pulled the headphones on.

Two hours later I was coming to the end of the job. There were a couple of singles that really stood out from this crop and I gave them five huge stars each. I saw Jade walk into the office and stride straight over towards me.

'I'm just finishing off,' I said, taking off the headphones.

'That's great,' she replied, 'but there's something else I need to talk to you about.'

OK, here it is. The storm cloud. She'd been a little bit kind to me and now it was time for savage cruelty.

'You're a big fan of Reel Love, right?'

I nodded hesitantly. Where was this going?

'Well I've just spoken to him. It's very eleventh hour, but he's doing a set at a club in Shoreditch called Sofa. He owes the manager a favour. Do you know the club?'

Did I know it? It's only one of the top clubs in Europe. Not that I'd ever been there.

'Yes.'

'How would you feel about being on the guest list?'

I stood up as if someone had just applied a red-hot poker to my backside.

'S . . . sorry?' I stammered.

'The guest list. Would you like to be on it?'

Letting me do a bit of work for her was one thing but this must be too good to be true. She must have sensed what I was thinking.

'I'm totally serious,' she said. 'He's doing a short, surprise set and you're in if you want to be.'

My facial expression yelled *WHY ME?*

'Look,' she went on, 'you trawl through the CD singles, I repay the favour by getting you in to see Reel Love. I think that's a reasonable exchange, don't you?'

'It's . . . amazing,' I said. 'Thanks.'

'No problem. Just look eighteen and get there by eight-thirty.'

A thought suddenly flashed through my mind.

'I know this is disgracefully cheeky, but is there any chance I could bring a couple of friends along?'

There was a brief pause, during which I envisaged all manner of negative responses to this request.

'Sure,' she replied, 'what are their names?'

As with all major activities of recent times, the face of Mum loomed large in my head. I'd calmed down a bit about the school party. I realised that if I constantly attacked her for banning me, then I'd get nowhere. I needed her on-side, especially now, so I'd been a lot less antagonistic towards her in the last few days. I hadn't yet mentioned the sports centre gig to her and now here I was on the guest list at Sofa! I didn't know how she'd feel about her fourteen-year-old daughter going clubbing. I could tell her we were going with Jade, but even that might not convince her. How crushed would I be if she said no to Sofa or the under-seventeen's gig, or even to both? I'd ask about Sofa as soon as I got home and, if that went according to plan, then later on I'd try and tackle Howie's gig.

Be bold, I told myself, and get straight to the point.

When I got in, I found Dad alone in the sitting room watching a music documentary.

'Where's Mum?' I asked casually.

'She's gone out with some women from work.'

'When will she back?'

'Don't know exactly. She told me not to wait up. Could be late.' His gaze drifted back to the TV.

I silently thanked the creature from the spirit world who was organising Mum's social life.

'Dad?'

He slowly turned back to face me.

I sat down next to him, pulled my cutest, most obedient child expression and began to explain the situation.

The door opened after my tenth knock. Keesha stared out at me. Becky stood moodily in the background. It was six-thirty and they certainly weren't expecting me.

'Can I come in?' I asked.

Keesha looked at me, trying to work out if I'd come as peace-maker or troublemaker. I should have worn a T-shirt declaring my intentions.

She must have decided on peacemaker because she waved her hand in front of her face to beckon me in.

I walked into the hall and stood in front of them. There was an awkward silence. Here were my two best mates and it felt like they were my sworn enemies. I'd had enough of the cold shoulder treatment. I wanted everything to be normal again.

'I've been a fool!' I shouted.

They looked at me as if I'd just gone completely mad.

'You were right! I've been so obsessed with music that I've neglected my mates. I've realised the error of my ways. I'm here to beg for forgiveness.'

I performed a dramatic bow.

It was Becky who cracked up first.

'You're crazy!' she shouted, throwing her arms round me. 'It's been miserable without you.'

Keesha gave me a side hug. 'We missed you and everything that goes with you – your jokes, your craziness, your fiendish brother!'

'Zoe's back!' Becky yelled as I managed to stop her squeezing me to death.

'We've tried to make each other laugh but we can't really do it without you,' said Keesha, smiling.

'We were also out of order,' said Becky, finally releasing me from her grasp. 'We shouldn't have had a go at you. If DJing is so important to you, we need to be a bit more interested in it, or at least act like we're a bit more interested.'

'Nothing's as important as you two,' I sung in a falsetto operatic voice.

We went up to Keesha's room, all talking at the same time.

When we got inside, I held my hands up for silence. It took a few seconds, but I managed to get them quiet.

'By way of an apology, I have a surprise outing planned for the three of us.'

They looked intrigued.

'Who's heard of Sofa?' I asked. 'And I don't mean the squashy thing you sit on with plumped up cushions.'

They looked at me with wide eyes.

'Who hasn't heard of it?' Keesha answered.

'This very night,' I told them, 'Reel Love just happens to be playing there. And I happen to know that a certain three girls are on the guest list.'

'No way!' squealed Becky.

'Way!' I shouted.

They both started jumping around the room screaming at the top of their voices and I thought it rude not to join them.

When we finally calmed down, I adopted a more serious tone.

'Mum was already out for the evening when I got home from CHILL so I sweet-talked Dad into it. He was in the middle of watching some music show on TV and said yes without too much prodding. He told me it was fine as long as I'm back by midnight at the very latest. He said he'd square it with Mum later.'

'My parents will be OK about it,' said Keesha.

'I'll stretch the truth with my mum,' Becky said, winking, 'and Dan will understand.'

'I'm really sorry I was such a pain,' I told them. 'I shouldn't have thrown you out. I over-reacted.'

'Forget that,' shouted Becky, 'we've got a top night out in a matter of hours and we haven't decided what to wear!'

'And we have to look eighteen to get in,' I reminded them.

'Don't worry,' screeched Keesha, sprinting over to her cupboard and flinging the door open. 'It's time for me to work some of my magic.'

It took me about half an hour to get ready. Keesha and Becky spent at least an hour. I was in a pair of Keesha's black leather trousers with a cropped white T-shirt and for once I wore my hair down. They both said I looked really good and on this occasion I had to agree with them. The person looking back at me from the mirror could pass as a relatively attractive eighteen-year-old.

Keesha was wearing her tartan miniskirt and a short-sleeved sequin top. Becky had a pair of boot-cut faded jeans and a baby blue halter-neck top. As we stood outside Keesha's house, Becky looked at the three of us approvingly.

'We look good!' she said.

'Rubbish!' shouted Keesha. 'We look *fantastic!*'

The queue for Sofa snaked right down the street and disappeared round the corner. It had taken us thirty minutes by bus to get to Shoreditch. A few people gave us dirty looks as we walked by. Their faces seemed to say, Don't even *think* about pushing in.

We got to the front of the queue where two massive, black-suited bouncers were standing blocking the entrance. I spoke to the one with a crocodile tattoo on his neck.

'Excuse me,' I began, 'we're on the guest list.'

He looked down at me as if I was some sort of slug that had just smeared slime on his shoes.

'Name?' he asked gruffly.

'Zoe Wynch.'

He spoke into the mouthpiece he was wearing and waited for a reply. He nodded seriously and for a few seconds I thought I was going to be turned away. But he gestured to his colleague and mouthed 'guest list'.

He ushered us forward, pulled back a rope and pointed us through a silver archway. Suddenly we were in.

'This is brilliant,' whispered Becky. 'It's like being a film star.'

We left our coats with the sulky girl in the cloakroom and walked down a narrow, dimly lit passage into a cavernous room. We were immediately hit by a giant wall of sound. A tune I knew was thumping out of the speakers and coloured lights flickered their rotating beams across the room. The place was overflowing with people. There was a bar all the way across the back wall and a dance floor in two rectangular sections, one on ground level and the other raised about a metre. It was a young crowd – mostly eighteen to twenty-five-year-olds I reckoned, and loads of people were dancing.

I looked at the DJ and saw at once that Reel Love wasn't on yet.

'I think this calls for a dance,' shouted Becky above the music. Keesha and me saw no reason to disobey this command and the three of us strode straight on to the upper dance floor.

The DJ was good and he played a decent mix of tracks. I knew most of them and as I danced I tried to predict which new tunes he'd cut in. After a few songs, we decided to take a break. We flopped down on to a low sofa next to the bar. We were busy raving to each other about what an amazing club it was, when I saw a familiar face.

It was Laura Tanner. She walked over to us through the mist of smoke and sat down on the edge of the sofa. She was wearing a low-cut dark blue dress.

'Fancy meeting you here,' she said with surprise. 'I thought you preferred life behind the decks.'

I grinned. 'I do, but I got an offer I couldn't refuse.'

'What do you mean?'

'We're on the guest list,' I replied with pride.

'You're joking!' she said with disbelief.

I shook my head.

'How on earth did you get on the guest list?' she asked. 'I've been here a couple of times before and it's, like, the most popular club in the country. Me and my mates waited for well over an hour to get in.'

'Someone at CHILL sorted it out – I work there on Saturdays.'

She looked seriously impressed and stood up to go, but before she went she looked at me.

'By the way,' she said, 'How's Zak?'

I rolled my eyes. 'Same as ever.'

She smiled in a wistful sort of way.

'He's not really a one-woman sort of guy is he?'

'That's one way of putting it.' I grinned.

Keesha laughed. 'He's unreal isn't he?'

Laura laughed, said goodbye and then disappeared into the crowd.

By ten-fifteen we were back on the dance floor and, a couple of minutes later, I got what I'd come for. The first DJ pulled off his headphones and made way for the main attraction. About thirty seconds later Reel Love strode into the DJ area to the sound of cheers and whistles, plugged in his headphones and started his set.

I WAS IN THE SAME ROOM AS REEL LOVE!

I made sure that I screamed louder than anyone else.

From the first track, he was unbelievable. And it was so much better hearing him live than on the radio. He played a mix of familiar and rare tunes, and the whole thing was so seamless. The crowd was going completely wild. I was totally into the music and kept on looking at the DJ booth to confirm that it really was him. We were no more than five metres away from him and we danced crazily for his whole set. I was tempted to get nearer to him but, even if I'd really wanted to, it would have been nearly impossible – the dance floor was that crowded.

This is the standard, I kept telling myself. It doesn't get any better. I thought about my capabilities and suddenly felt seriously worried. Tomorrow morning Dan and Howie might get a nasty shock when they came and listened to my mini-set. Compared to Reel Love, I was nothing. Hang on a second, I told myself, you're obviously nowhere near as good as him, but he's had years of practice to get where he is.

Reel Love did about an hour and, halfway through his last track, he stepped back and waved to the crowd. The noise in response was deafening. I was waving, jumping and yelling all at the same time.

And then he was gone.

The other guy stepped back in.

'What did I tell you?' I shouted at Keesha and Becky. 'The guy's a genius.

They both nodded in agreement. We were exhausted and elated.

We saw Laura again at the cloakroom and were about to launch into a huge rant about how brilliant Reel Love was, but she looked really upset.

'Are you OK?' I asked.

She shook her head. 'I've just seen something really nasty.'

'What?' asked Becky.

'There's a whole load of us here tonight,' she explained, 'and we reckon this girl Kathy had her drink spiked.'

'How do you know?' Keesha asked.

'We left our drinks and went for a dance – we were only away from the table for ten minutes. Soon after we came back, she had a drink and suddenly went all drowsy. We tried to talk to her but she was really out of it – seemed like she'd lost control. We reckon it was one of those date-rape drugs, like Rohypnol.'

'That's terrible,' Keesha said.

I shivered. The excitement of Reel Love's set had instantly vanished.

'Does anyone know who did it?' Becky asked.

'No idea,' Laura replied. 'Kathy can't remember anything, so no one knows how much she drank. Thank God there were loads of us with her, otherwise anything could have happened.'

'Is she going to be OK?' I asked.

'A couple of her mates have taken her to casualty at St Helens – to get her checked out.'

Keesha looked appalled. 'It's disgusting that some creep could do something like that.'

Becky nodded and looked over her shoulder. 'It could have been anyone here.'

I looked back into the club. It didn't seem so glamorous and appealing now. I'd read stuff about those drugs that knock you out, make you compliant and unable to fight back.

'It's a real warning,' Laura added. 'Never let a drink out of your sight.'

We said goodbye to her before we got our coats from the cloakroom.

'I can't believe it,' Becky said. 'Some people are totally evil.'

Keesha and me nodded as we stepped outside the club. Next

time I went anywhere near a club, I'd be sure to carry my drink with me at all times.

'Hope she's OK,' said Keesha.

The queue outside was still huge, but the three of us were really shocked about the spiked drink and we weren't in the mood anymore to celebrate our guest-list status.

A bus drove into view after about five minutes and we hardly talked on the journey home. We were all thinking about Kathy and how it so easily could have been one of us.

Chapter 23 . DJ Zed and the fantastic flyer

Howie and Dan sat on my bed, nodding their heads in time with the music. Thankfully, Mum had gone over to a friend who was in the process of a messy divorce and needed a shoulder to cry on. It bought me a few extra hours. Dad poked his head round the door, but just nodded and left.

As I was finishing my mini-set, I had no idea from their expressions what Dan and Howie were thinking. Was I good? Or couldn't they wait to escape from the noise pollution I was serving them? I faded the last track and put my headphones down.

'Well?' I asked nervously.

They both looked at me.

Dan grinned. 'I told you she was good.'

Keesha and Becky knew that Dan and Howie were coming over to mine to check out my mixing skills — they really wanted me to get the sports centre gig. Keesha seemed to be totally over Tim and Becky and Dan were getting on great. She'd told me that

Dan had begun standing up to her more and she liked it.

'You're better than good,' said Howie, nodding as the last beat faded from the speakers. 'You've got yourself a gig. Fifty quid OK with you?'

I got home from Sofa the night before at five to twelve.

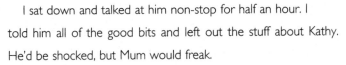

Dad was reading a book in the kitchen.

'How did it go?' he asked.

I sat down and talked at him non-stop for half an hour. I told him all of the good bits and left out the stuff about Kathy. He'd be shocked, but Mum would freak.

Mum had really enjoyed her night out, and arrived home at two in the morning, which is amazingly late for her. When Dad told her at breakfast about me going to Sofa, she seemed remarkably OK about it. I knew I had to broach the subject of Howie's party with her, but I wasn't sure when a good moment would be. She had to say yes. A 'no' was unthinkable.

Over the last few days Zak had been busy seeing Claire and no doubt several other girls, but I talked to him at every opportunity about the new gig. He promised to back me up when I told Mum and Dad.

There was a real buzz around school about the sports centre gig. Word was spreading that I was the DJ and a few older kids thought it was funny to mock this fourteen-year-old girl. But they got as good as they gave – from me, and of course from Keesha and Becky.

On the Monday I floated around school in a haze. My mind leapt from Reel Love's set to the spiked drink and back again. During lunch break, Ms Devlin caught me in the school canteen.

'Hi Zoe,' she said. 'How are you doing?'

'OK,' I replied.

She sat down at a table and pointed to another chair. I sat opposite her.

'How are things with Keesha and Becky?'

'It's sorted. You were right about them.'

'And your mum?' she asked.

I thought about this for a minute.

'Things are a bit better – we're on speaking terms.'

Ms Devlin smiled. 'I've been thinking about what you said the other day – about trying to find the right balance in your life and all that university stuff.'

'What do you think?' I enquired. 'That I'm a teenage freak who should be locked in a cage until she's got over her "difficult" years?'

She laughed. 'Of course not. And I can't do anything about you achieving a suitable balance in your life. That's totally up to you. But I can help you start to think about your future and be armed with the most up-to-date information.'

'What sort of information?' I asked.

She reached down into her bag and pulled out several sheets of paper.

'These are print-outs from the internet. I looked for university and college courses that were straight music or music-orientated.'

She pushed the papers across the table and I started flicking through them.

'This is fantastic,' I said enthusiastically, poring over the words as if I'd just won a suitcase of gold bars. 'I can't believe how many courses are out there. Look, there's even a music production course that has a module on DJing!'

'And just remember that's what's available now,' she replied. 'Think of what there may be a few years down the road.'

'Can I keep these?' I asked.

'Of course. They're for you.'

She stood up to go.

'It's really good of you to check this all out for me,' I said standing, with one eye still scanning the print-outs. In spite of Mum being OK about my night at Sofa, I still needed whatever ammunition I could get to make her even a tiny bit more positive towards my DJing.

'It was nothing,' she said. 'It only took twenty minutes.'

Five minutes after I got in from school, I was studying Ms Devlin's print-outs when Dan showed up. He stood on the doorstep with a wide grin.

'What are you so happy about?' I asked.

He reached inside his jacket pocket and pulled out a piece of paper. It was a flyer for the sports centre party. The words *DJ Zed* were strung along the top in thick black letters.

'This is the first batch, hot off the press,' Dan said.

'They're fantastic!' I squealed, hugging him.

'Hey,' he said laughing and then, pulling away after a few seconds, 'I designed them myself. Do you like them?'

'Like them?' I yelled at him. 'They're the greatest flyers I've ever been on. Actually they're the only flyers I've ever been on, but who cares?'

'Too right!' he said patting me on the shoulder. 'How many do you need?'

At that moment I heard Mum's voice calling from the study.

'What's all the fuss about?' she demanded.

I remembered that she and Dad knew nothing about the sports centre gig.

'I'll take five!' I whispered quickly.

He counted them out and handed them over.

'Great!' I said. 'Got to go.'

I shut the front door hurriedly. Poor Dan. One minute he's the greatest person on earth, the next he has a door slammed in his face.

I heard Mum's footsteps on the stairs and quickly hid the flyers under my T-shirt.

'Is Dad in?' I asked.

'He's watching telly,' she replied. 'Why?'

'Can I talk to both of you?' I said.

'OK' she said. 'Let's go to the kitchen.'

'Tony!' she shouted. 'Zoe wants to talk to us.'

I heard the TV being switched off. Dad came into the kitchen.

'Everything OK?' he asked.

'Everything's fine,' I responded. 'There's a couple of things I need to talk to you about.'

'Shoot,' he said, pulling up a chair. Mum stood, leaning against the fridge.

I cleared my throat.

'You know you've been going on about university?' I addressed this point directly to Mum. 'Well I've been doing some research. Or rather Ms Devlin's been doing some research on my behalf. She's given me some info about music courses. In universities and colleges.'

I handed the print-outs to Mum. Dad stood up, moved across the kitchen and leaned over her shoulder. They spent a couple of minutes looking over the papers.

'Some of these look great,' Dad murmured enthusiastically. 'I didn't know you could do so many different courses.'

I waited for Mum's reaction nervously.

'That's the whole point,' I explained. 'Even though university's not for a few years, you were right – there's no harm in checking out all of the options. You see, I can study some sort of music and media degree. There doesn't have to be this strict divide between studying and DJing.'

At last Mum spoke.

'Can you leave these with me?'

'Sure,' I replied, 'keep them for as long as you like.'

In my head I thanked Ms Devlin for bothering to turn her computer on and print out the music course details for me. Mum was definitely interested in them. Maybe this information could form part of a package that would swing Mum slightly more in favour of Zoe Wynch also being DJ Zed.

'What was the other thing?' Dad asked. 'You said there were a couple of things.'

'Oh yeah,' I replied, 'it's . . . I've just . . . I want . . .' I couldn't quite order my words in a coherent way.

'Go on,' said Dad. 'Tell us.'

Come on, Zoe, I urged myself. Straight out with it.

'I've been asked to DJ at a party organised by Dan's older brother Howie. It's going to be at a sports centre. It's an under-seventeen's gig. Please let me do it – I swear I'll be the most devoted student in the northern hemisphere if you say yes.'

Mum looked at me with pursed lips. I couldn't read her facial expression. Was it positive? Was it negative? Or had she just stubbed her toe?

Dad looked at Mum.

Mum looked at me.

There was an agonising pause.

'You can do it,' said Mum.

I checked my ears to determine if they were working properly.

'Sorry?'

'You can do it.'

'Just like that?'

'Just like that.'

Mum must have seen from my total shock that she needed to do a bit of explaining.

'I know you think I'm totally against your DJ stuff, but I'm not. I've just got your best interests at heart – I don't want you to give up on school for a dream that may never happen. You've been making much more of an effort with your schoolwork, so it's only fair that you can do this party.'

I felt guilty about all of those times I'd been in my room pretending to do my homework. But that feeling only lasted about five seconds.

I screamed 'thank you' repeatedly and ran around the kitchen like a headless chicken.

Mum laughed. 'Go and tell the world before I change my mind.'

I sped out of the kitchen and ran upstairs. This called for celebration phone calls. I had to tell Keesha and Becky. But before I even reached the phone, a thought suddenly occurred to me.

I grabbed my jacket and shouted to my parents that I was popping out for twenty minutes.

Rix shook his head with complete disinterest when I asked if the American imports had come in.

'I told you it could take ages,' he sneered. 'Sometimes you order things and they never show. So be prepared for disappointment. The package may have been lost in transit.'

That was Rix for you – always a cheery voice to jolly you along.

I reached into my pocket and pulled out one of Dan's flyers.

'I was wondering if you'd put one of these up,' I said, holding the flyer a few centimetres from Rix's face. He lifted it out of my hand and studied it for a few seconds. His lips quickly formed into a smirk.

'What is this?' he smirked. 'Some sort of children's party? Why don't you go to the kids play centre? They'll put it up for you.'

Rix ambled off, and I stared at him as he pulled on his head-phones and started playing a hip-hop track on the Tune Spin system. I usually ignored Rix's taunts, but for some reason this put-down really got to me.

I edged across the shop, pretending to look at some funk twelve-inches. I kneeled down slowly, keeping my eyes on Rix all the time. He was grinning – probably congratulating himself on being the finest DJ within a twelve-mile radius. Without hesitation, I pulled out the system's plug socket. Suddenly Rix's tune went dead and the mixer shut down.

He glared across the shop and saw me standing up next to the socket. He looked completely furious. But I didn't care. It was high time for a fight-back and I strode towards the door, feeling assertive and powerful. I turned back quickly to check his reaction.

For once in that sphere of sourness, otherwise known as Rix's life, something remarkable was taking place. There was no put-down or wisecrack.

The guy was completely speechless.

Chapter 24 . Backflips and Somersaults

My alarm went and, in the twilight zone between fast asleep and partially awake, I vaguely remembered that something special was on the horizon. It didn't take long for my brain to kick into gear. Oh yes, it was the most important day of my life. As the day had approached I felt my nerves jangling increasingly wildly inside me. I'd made sure that I kept my mixing practice to a minimum and schoolwork to a maximum – even though I wanted to spend every second of every day at my decks. I'd also reined myself in with Keesha and Becky. I didn't want to overdo the whole music thing and fall out with them again. I needn't have worried though. They'd been absolutely brilliant – really encouraging me and even looking at my set list.

For the only time in living memory, I was the first person up on a Saturday. When Dad came down he was amazed to find me sitting at the kitchen table eating breakfast.

'Is your bed broken?' he asked, wiping the sleep out of his eyes.

'Hilarious!' I said with a snort. 'But wrong. Today is filled with possibilities.'

He stopped in front of the fridge and eyed me warily.

'Have you been drinking Mum's sherry?'

'Tune in, Dad,' I said, twirling my cereal spoon in the air, 'tonight is my night behind the decks.'

'Of course!' he said, plucking a milk bottle out of the fridge. 'The big one.'

'Not the big one,' I protested. 'Think *massive, gigantic, humungous . . .*'

'How could I forget?' He laughed. 'It reminds me of my first gig. It was in an old church hall. I was unbelievably nervous. I paced up and down for hours before we played. The funny thing was, only two people showed up. And one of them was my best mate. I couldn't believe it. My mate stayed for the whole thing, but the other bloke left after ten minutes.'

'Thanks for the motivational story! Any more inspiring tales from the world of music?' I asked sarcastically.

He shook his head.

'OK then, I'll be up in my room if anyone needs me.'

I walked upstairs. After hours of thought I'd finally decided in which order to play my records at tonight's gig. Well, nearly.

'How early is embarrassing?' I was walking up and down in my room. My level of nervousness had been rising sharply all day. I wouldn't be on for another four hours, but I was already just a short step away from Completely Hysterical.

Keesha and Becky were sitting on my bed. They'd been amazingly patient with me as I'd been talking at great speed for almost the whole two hours they'd been there.

'Do you mean embarrassingly embarrassing or just embarrassing?' asked Becky as she flicked through a fashion mag.

'What's the difference?' asked Keesha.

But before Becky could start on any lengthy definitions, I jumped in.

'You know what I mean. Just tell me. What time?'

'It officially starts at eight,' noted Keesha, studying the flyer, 'What time are you on?'

'Nine,' I said, trying to sound normal and not ultra-nervous.

'How about getting there at seven-thirty?' Keesha asked.

I shook my head. 'Not enough time. How about six-thirty?'

'That *would* be embarrassingly embarrassing,' answered Becky, looking up from an article in *Future Femme* magazine, entitled *How to Make Your Feet Look More Attractive in Five Easy Steps.*

'OK,' I said, 'let's compromise on seven.'

'Sounds good,' Becky replied.

'Then that's settled,' said Keesha.

'How are the nerves?' asked Becky, studying her ankles carefully.

'Worsening by the second,' I replied, jogging on the spot to burn off some excess energy.

'What shall I wear?' This was my next brainteaser for the girls.

We took out everything from my wardrobe and laid all of my

clothes on the bed and across the floor. It took us forty minutes to reach a final decision and that was only after a two to one vote, with me and Keesha overriding Becky.

I went for a pair of faded jeans, a white T-shirt with a black *Mix It!* logo and a pair of trainers.

'What about my hair?' I enquired, playing with it. 'Up, down, shave it all off for tonight?'

Keesha laughed. 'Hair down is very rock chic.'

'Cool rock chic though,' added Becky.

I grimaced. 'Come on you two, this is important.'

'The trouble with down is HIF,' said Becky thoughtfully.

'What's that?' I groaned.

'Hair In Face – it could seriously interfere with your mixing abilities.'

'Yeah,' nodded Keesha, 'definitely up.'

'With a clip,' said Becky, throwing me one from my bedside table.

I pulled my hair up and studied myself in the mirror. Did I look like a proper DJ? Or just like some teenage imposter who was about to be found out?

'What do you reckon?' I asked, turning to face them.

'Spot on!' Becky said, beaming, while Keesha gave me a thumbs-up.

They'd brought all of their gear over and after a fleeting panic over Keesha's lost make-up bag, by ten to seven we were ready. Keesha was wearing a short black dress and long black boots. Becky was in a denim skirt with a tight, black, short-sleeved lace V-neck top.

'I think it's time to go,' said Becky.

My nerves upped a gear. This was it – there was no going back.

I nodded and had one last glance in the mirror.

OK, I told myself, you look fine. Now all you need to do is get the music right.

Zack appeared from his room to wish me the best – he was coming along later and would see us there.

As we walked downstairs towards the front door, Mum appeared from the kitchen, smiling at me. 'Good luck, Zoe. Hope it all goes brilliantly.'

I grinned back at her. Despite all of our recent arguments and fights, I knew she meant it.

Howie and Dan were waiting at the doors of the sports centre when we arrived. There were two bouncers standing with their arms folded. They weren't quite as bulky as the guys at Sofa, but they weren't far off.

'You look fantastic,' Dan said, marvelling at Becky.

She beamed and nodded towards Keesha and me.

'You two also look great,' he added on cue.

'Right,' said Howie, directing me away from the others, 'let me show you round.'

I left Dan, Keesha and Becky talking by the doors and followed Howie towards a sign saying Main Hall. We went through and, as soon as I stepped inside, I froze with awe. I'd been in there a couple of times before, once for a sports day and another time, years ago, for a friend's party. All I could remember was a big room with wooden wall bars along one side.

But the place had been totally transformed. There were slide projectors filtering all sorts of wacky images on the walls – a giant unicycle, a troupe of circus clowns and a cartoon camel – to name but a few. The lighting system was brilliant – a mesh of colours and textures. Huge pieces of glittery material hung from the ceiling.

'You must have spent a fortune,' I whispered to Howie. 'It looks brilliant.'

He smiled proudly.

'My dad lent me five hundred quid,' he admitted, 'and said I can pay him back when I've made enough cash from doing these gigs. I've already broken even for tonight and there are quite a few tickets left, so I'll make a bit of a profit. I reckon by my third or fourth one, I'll be able to pay Dad back and not need any help to carry on doing them.'

The mixing decks were set up on a small stage at the far side of the hall. We walked over to them and I saw a sound guy crouching down at the base of the stage, connecting some wires.

'What do you think?' asked Howie, a little nervously.

I climbed on to the stage and scanned the mixing desk and the decks. Then I checked out the speakers dotted round the room. It was without question a first-class set up.

'Fantastic,' I murmured.

He turned to the sound guy.

'Phil, this is Zoe.'

Phil looked up for a second and then returned to his wires. 'If it's about food,' he said, 'I'm OK. I've eaten already.'

'Zoe's the DJ tonight,' said Howie sharply.

Phil turned and looked at me with surprise. He reddened slightly and dropped a cable. 'I wasn't expecting a . . . you know . . . a girl. I thought you were doing the catering.'

'Welcome to the modern world,' said Howie, side-stepping any tension and slapping Phil on the back.

Phil managed a thin smile. 'Yeah, cool, whatever.' He finished twisting some speaker cable and then went off.

Phil's comments were annoying but I didn't let them get to me. I was too busy gaping round the room. I felt a knot in my stomach tighten. After hundreds of hours of bedroom practice, this was the night I'd been waiting for.

'Right,' Howie said, jumping down from the stage, 'I've got to head back to the front. If you need anything, give Dan a shout. He'll come and get me.'

'No problem,' I said. 'Thanks.'

He sped off and headed out of the hall.

I was alone.

I stood behind the decks for a couple of minutes, looking around me, trying to imagine what the hall might look like mid-party when the place was full. It felt a bit overwhelming . . .

What was I thinking of? How could I possibly do a set in front of all of these people? I should have said no when Dan told me about the gig. I should stick strictly to bedroom performances.

Get a grip, Zoe, I commanded myself. Use this time properly. Get a feel for the system.

I carefully started unloading my twelve-inches on to the table at the right side of the decks. The table was empty save for a small stand holding a microphone. I pushed it to the far end of the table. I certainly wouldn't be doing any talking. I pulled my headphones out of my record bag and plugged them in. I reached for the latest Reel Love single and dropped it on to the first deck. I tried it first in the headphones, just to check the system was actually up and running. Reassured that all was in good working order, I steered the up fader and the tune began playing out of the speakers.

A few seconds later, Dan stuck his head round the door.

'Sounds great!' he shouted.

His encouraging words gave me a tiny bit of confidence.

At five past eight a few eager party-goers started trickling into the room. Howie scooted up and handed me a dance mix CD. The party had officially begun, but I could see that it was going to take a while to heat up.

'Stick that on, Zoe, and go and get a drink. Relax. Remember, you're not on till nine.'

I flicked on the CD and went off in search of Keesha and Becky.

They were at the bar, which was situated in a far smaller room next door to the main hall. They were chatting to Dan and some of his mates.

'The main attraction!' shouted Becky. 'Ladies and gentlemen, tonight's DJ is the one and only Zoe Wynch!'

A few people around her clapped. I blushed deeply and walked over to join them.

'Did you have to?' I asked her.

'You know I did,' Becky whispered. 'Me and Keesha are best mates with the star of the show. We want everyone to know.'

A couple of Dan's friends asked me about how I'd got into DJing and what gigs I'd done before. I answered the first question and managed to side-step the second.

I hung around with them for about twenty minutes or so but, however hard I tried to relax, I could feel my stomach bubbling with nerves. Forget butterflies, there was a whole *bees' nest* in there.

'How ya doing?' asked Keesha, putting her arm round my shoulders and dragging me away from Dan's friends, who by now were quizzing me about the sound system.

'I'm fine,' I replied, 'terrified but fine.'

'What's there to be terrified of?' she asked. 'The set up looks superb and you know what you're doing. You're going to be brilliant.'

'Do you really think so?' I asked nervously.

'I don't think so. I *know* so. You're going to get up there and blow people's minds.'

Becky joined us and saw my anxious expression. 'Don't let your nerves stop you having fun, Zoe. Just enjoy it.'

And in that instant, I suddenly knew they were right. I couldn't let myself get so nervous that I had a terrible time. After all, the countless mixing sessions in my bedroom had all been about tonight – the chance to play in front of a live audience.

Suddenly I heard a slight eruption of noise from the far side of the room. I tensed as I watched Gail and Josh enter and make their way to the bar. Gail was screeching 'hello's' to every person she knew and to several she didn't.

Keesha squeezed my elbow supportively.

'Don't let them make you lose your focus,' she commanded. 'They're irrelevant. Tonight is about you and the music.'

'Hey, you can be my life coach,' I said, laughing. 'How much do you charge an hour?'

She smiled.

'Only doing my job, Zoe.'

Gail and Josh wandered off. I carried on talking to Keesha and Becky while my stomach carried on snowboarding. At ten to nine, Dan hurried over to me carrying a plastic bag.

'Some guy left these for you with one of the bouncers.'

I looked at him with bewilderment. I reached inside the bag and pulled out two twelve-inch records. Or more specifically two *imported American* twelve-inch records. I held them out in front of me for a few seconds. Rix! Could it really be that the bane of my life had hand-delivered them here? Surely it wasn't possible? But I had the proof right there in my hands. I didn't have much time to dwell on this incredibly freaky news because, by now, people were arriving in big numbers.

I surveyed the crowd. There were some people I knew from

school, plus loads of unfamiliar faces. I was watching as the room started really filling up when I felt a tap on my arm. It was Howie. I felt my whole insides performing backflips and somersaults as he struggled to make himself heard above the noise.

'It's nearly nine, Zoe. You're on.'

Chapter 15 . Freak Out

Tania: *You come across as supremely confident, Zoe, but surely you can't be like that all of the time?*

Zoe: *Of course I'm not, Tania. There isn't a performer on earth who doesn't suffer from some type of stage fright. Some gigs are particularly terrifying, particularly if your best friends and the boy you're crazy about are going to be in the crowd.*

Tania: *So how do you calm your nerves?*

Zoe: *I find that placing kiwi segments over my eyes and listening to a CD of beach pebbles can be very helpful.*

Tania: *And what's this I hear about goat's milk? Sounds a bit Cleopatra-ish.*

Zoe: *I know, it is rather outrageous, but I've found it works. Bathing in it is a delightful and calming experience. And if you're hungry you can just throw in some cereal and, hey presto, you have a healthy snack.*

Tania: *Fascinating.*

Zoe: *Of course, the other thing you can do is leap around your* *dressing room screaming: 'I'VE NEVER BEEN SO SCARED!' That always brings someone running who'll be happy to 'talk you down'.*

Tania: *So what advice would you have for aspiring performers who are hit by stage fright?*

Zoe: *Your first show is probably your most frightening. I recommend closing your eyes when you get on stage. Then you don't have to actually see the audience.*

Tania: *But what happens if you're, for example, a knife thrower in a circus act?*

Zoe: *That's a difficult one. All I would say is make sure you practise a lot.*

'Go for it.'

I looked at Howie's excited face and gazed at the crowd standing around expectantly. There were about a hundred people. And they were all looking at me. The last notes of the dance CD faded.

I was now in sole control of the music.

I pinched myself on my left arm. A bit too hard, because it hurt quite a lot, but it helped. I was here. It was real. I was the DJ.

'Do you want me to introduce you?' Howie whispered, pointing to the microphone.

I shook my head and pulled on my headphones.

'I'll let the music do the talking,' I replied.

Cheesy, I know. Yet somehow appropriate.

He stood back and let me get on with it.

I moved the needle across and lightly placed it on the Reel Love record. It had to be the first tune – there was no contest.

The first sixteen beats thundered out of the speakers and the bassline kicked in.

Keesha, Becky, Dan and a couple of his mates were near the stage and immediately started dancing. Within about a minute more bodies were moving. But the vast majority of the crowd were still stationary, as if they were judging me.

Five minutes in and my hands were shaking as I touched the cross fader for the first mix. There were more like two hundred people now and the vast majority weren't dancing. I was gripped by panic. Why weren't people dancing? What if I messed up the mix? What if it sounded like an annoying kid messing about with a broken toy stereo? What if the crowd started swearing at me and throwing objects in my direction?

There was only one way to find out.

I pulled the cross fader delicately over and ever so slowly brought in the second track.

I'd done my preparation well. The beats were aligned and it sounded promising.

Go on, Zoe, I urged myself, do it!

I pulled the fader further across and brought up the volume on the second tune, while simultaneously pulling down the first. I was concentrating so hard that my fingers felt like they were stuck to the faders. I looked down at the mixing desk and then across at the crowd.

Keep going, Zoe, I urged myself, it's almost there.

Fifteen seconds later and the deed was done.

The first tune was dust.

The mix was complete.

It had gone OK. Not perfect, but definitely good enough.

More people were spilling into the hall. A few more had begun to dance and this gave me a boost of energy.

The second mix was a fraction tighter and there was a tiny smattering of applause, naturally generated by Keesha, Becky and Dan. I willed more people to dance, but there was still a large part of the crowd that seemed to be unmoved by the tunes I was playing.

What would happen if most people left the room, leaving a tiny crowd behind? I could see myself on the front page of the local paper under the enormous headline – TEENAGE DJ FAILS TO MAKE PEOPLE DANCE!

Come on, I told myself, stop being so negative. You're two mixes in and so far nobody has attempted to burn the sound system.

The third mix received a slightly louder round of applause (by now it had spread beyond my three admirers). But there were still far too many people standing around chatting. I formed an equation in my head: very few dancers equals rubbish DJ.

I'd just faded in the next tune when a big guy with wafer thin glasses and a ponytail approached the stage and requested a record. I quickly explained it was a no-requests set.

He stared at me with disbelief.

'What sort of a DJ doesn't do requests?' he asked.

'The best sort,' piped up Howie, miraculously appearing at my side. 'Now stop hassling the DJ and clear off.'

I felt bad for a few seconds. Perhaps people wanted a request-playing DJ. Maybe I was arrogant in thinking that everyone would like the music I was playing.

But Howie must have seen the doubt on my face because he squeezed my arm.

'You're doing great!' he beamed. 'Keep it up.'

The request boy sloped off and I carried on working the records. Still there were people arriving. By now there must have been well over three hundred. Why were so many of them still not dancing? Were they suffering from recently acquired sports injuries? Or was there some sort of glue smeared on large parts of the hall floor?

It was then that I happened to spot Gail and Josh dancing closely together and experienced a sensation of intense jealousy.

Forget about Josh and Gail, I instructed myself. This is your night. Ignore them.

What could I do to get these people dancing? I looked down at my set list and groaned. I'd picked the finest tunes in the perfect order, but things weren't going to plan. I looked around the room again. And then it suddenly struck me.

Forget the set list. Forget the order. This crowd needed a good musical kick up the backside. I frantically rummaged through my record bag and pulled out a twelve-inch in a funky turquoise cover.

It was a Latino tune with amazing beats. It was much more mainstream than most of my other stuff, but maybe this could do the trick. Perhaps a familiar tune would get to them.

As I dropped the record on to the deck, I thought that this was maybe my last chance to redeem myself. If the majority of people didn't start dancing soon, the gig would turn out to be a total catastrophe and I'd be the laughing stock of north London. I lined the Latino track up. This was a totally crucial moment for me and the whole party. Please work, please work, please work.

As I cut it in, for a few seconds nothing in the crowd changed and then suddenly it was as if someone had cranked the dance floor on to full power. The whole room burst into life and twenty seconds later I could hardly see anyone who wasn't dancing. I stared out at the mass of people with utter surprise and delight. A couple of people had brought whistles and they were blowing them in time with the tune. The whole atmosphere in the room had changed in less than a minute from stifled awkwardness to mad party scene.

After the Latino record I played another fast tune with a thundering bassline.

A minute into the track there were some loud cheers from the dance floor. I allowed myself a tiny smile. Maybe the night wouldn't turn out so disastrously.

As I felt my heart pounding with excitement, I rooted around in my record bag – crazily grabbing twelve-inches. My set list was toast. I'd play anything to keep the crowd dancing.

And things did step up a gear with the arrival of each new track. What started with a few isolated whoops of encouragement became loud roars of appreciation. The dance floor was packed with people going wild.

Going wild to my music! In spite of the amazing electricity I felt inside my body, I knew I was slowly starting to relax.

Forty-five minutes into my set and I was feeling even better. There was a massive welcome for each new tune. I couldn't believe it.

They were enjoying it.

I was enjoying it!

I started dancing behind the decks in between mixes, waving my arms frantically in the air and singing along with each track. I must have looked crazy but I didn't care.

I picked out Keesha, Becky and Dan who were dancing madly, and waved to them. They screamed their approval and waved back.

By ten o'clock I was on a total high. Each mix seemed to get better and the dance floor was heaving with dancers having an amazing time.

Howie appeared next to me again. 'How are you feeling?' he asked.

'Think of heaven,' I shouted, leaping about in front of him, 'and multiply it by a thousand.'

And that was a fair assessment of how I felt: joyous beyond words.

'Wind it down in five,' Howie instructed me. 'First rule of any gig. Always end on a high.'

'I'm fine,' I insisted. 'Let me carry on.'

The thought of stopping was unbearable, but I knew Howie was right. There was no way I wanted to overstay my welcome, even though that was highly unlikely given the crowd's fantastic response to my set.

'I'll do one more,' I shouted at him.

He looked at me and grinned.

'You're the DJ.'

As the last tune faded, Howie grabbed the mike and yelled, 'Let's hear it for the one and only – DJ Zed.'

Howie raised his arms in the air and clapped thunderously.

There was an almighty cheer from the dance floor and cries of 'More!'

'They loved you!' yelled Howie, passing me a CD. 'You were fantastic!'

I turned on the CD, walked away from the decks and stepped off the stage. Within seconds Becky was jumping on me and hugging me while simultaneously screaming in my right ear.

'You were unbelievable,' she shrieked, with no regard for my eardrum. 'Everyone thought so. Not just us. Everyone. There were complete strangers saying how good you were.'

Dan was at my side. 'You were awesome,' he shouted. 'The best DJ I've ever seen.'

Loads of his mates were there too, shouting their congratulations. It was the most amazing ego trip I'd ever experienced, at least since winning an under-sevens fancy dress contest when Mum dressed me up as a mushroom. It seemed that, whichever way I turned, someone else was there congratulating me. It was weird. A couple of hours ago, I'd been this terrified person afraid of screwing up. Now, I was being lauded as the next big thing to hit the club scene.

After about ten minutes of this, my back was stinging from constantly being slapped and I decided if anyone else touched me, I'd whack them.

'Where's Keesha?' I yelled at Becky.

'No idea,' she said, shrugging her shoulders, 'she was here a few minutes ago.'

I looked around, but there was no sign of her.

Howie turned up the volume of the CD and lots of people started dancing again.

'Just going to escape for a bit,' I yelled at Becky.

She raised her hand to slap me on the back, but saw my forbidding expression. She retracted her hand and mouthed, 'See you later.'

I made it through the thicket of people, with several dancers nodding at me or shouting their approval. I left the main hall and walked into the bar where it was pretty quiet, then headed over to get a bottle of water.

My ears were ringing from the music (and from Becky's yelling) but I couldn't stop smiling. After all of those pre-set nerves, I'd pulled it off. No one could take it away from me. I'd just done my first proper gig.

I was still hot from doing my set and I decided to get some fresh air. I walked away from the main hall, down the corridor and past the toilets with their cheap neon lights. Past the caretaker's office. Along a dimly lit passage ending in a door that opened to the outside. I stepped towards the door, edging past two people locked in a passionate embrace. I wouldn't have taken a second look at them, but they were illuminated by a thin shaft of blue light.

And I immediately regretted being there.

One of them was Zak. The other was Keesha.

Chapter 16 · Three Degrees of Love

I walked around to the front of the building from the side exit, after nearly tripping over Zak and Keesha. Luckily, they'd been too involved to notice me. I leaned against the whitewashed wall and let the cool night air hit my cheeks. It contrasted sharply with the intense heat my body was producing. The yellowy-orange light of the sports centre car park gave the forecourt a hazy glow.

One of the bouncers, a massive guy, was standing impassively as a couple of young kids tried unsuccessfully to get past him and make it inside to the party.

'I'm sixteen,' shouted the boy who wasn't a day over eleven.

'Me too,' claimed the girl who looked like she'd only just graduated from nursery.

'Go and bother someone else,' barked the bouncer gruffly, 'or I'll phone your parents.'

They didn't seem to like this and skulked off miserably into the shadows.

As I watched this scene unfold, I thought about what I'd just seen. My wayward brother snogging one of my best mates.

It was almost impossible to believe. In fact, if I hadn't witnessed it personally and someone had told me about it, I'd have accused them of lying.

I tried to be rational, but it looked the same from every angle: *brother and best mate. Snogging.*

It felt totally weird. Keesha had so often been there when I'd broadcast warnings about Zak and his ever-changing girlfriend rota. Why hadn't she listened to my advice?

Then something else struck me. What if this wasn't the first time they'd snogged? What if they'd been seeing each other behind my back? I didn't think it could be serious – nothing with Zak ever was – but what if Keesha really liked him? She'd only recently been dumped by Tim and now she could be getting involved with a serial let-downer. Maybe she was on the rebound and Zak seemed like a knight in shining armour? He was a good listener and maybe that's what Keesha was looking for.

I just stood there, rooted to the spot, feeling shocked and confused.

After about fifteen minutes, a very tall guy with multiple earrings walked out of the building and saw me by the wall.

'Brilliant set!' he called to me as he headed off to unlock his scooter.

I stopped thinking about Zak and Keesha for a minute and thought about how well my set had gone. No. It had gone *brilliantly* –

better than I could have ever imagined. All of my fears about being a fraud and a disaster had been unfounded. The hours of practice in my bedroom had paid off. People loved my music and hadn't been shy about telling me. Loads of them had been *cheering* for me.

It was a massive adrenalin rush, doing the gig, and surely there was nothing stopping me, right? The only way was up. Then I suddenly thought back to what Jade had told me about being female in a male-orientated industry . . . all of those bookers, promoters, club owners . . . the put-downs and comments made by people like the sound guy, Phil.

But then I remembered the American imports. They were still in a plastic bag next to the sound system. I'd left them there during my set and forgotten all about them. Rude, arrogant, patronising Rix, who never missed a chance to humiliate me, had brought them to *my* gig. Why?

My mind started racing. It kept jumping between visions of Keesha and Zak and the experiences of the last few weeks . . . I flashed back to Reel Love's gig at Sofa. He'd been incredible, but I was totally freaked out about Kathy and the spiked drink. How many sleazebags were out there in clubland waiting to do the same thing? Was this a world I really wanted to work in?

And then there was Mum. She'd shown interest in Ms Devlin's print-outs, but would a few course details off the internet persuade her that I could include DJing in my life without jeopardising all other aspects of my development? Or would she keep on at me insistently, until the only way to get her off my back was to bin my sound system or emigrate to New Zealand?

As my mind zipped through all these things, I stood alone outside the sports centre and felt a whole mixture of feelings at the same time: elation, anger, disbelief, betrayal, satisfaction, relief, sorrow, concern. I was a walking container of emotional extremes and I was so busy trying to deal with all of these that at first I didn't hear my name being called.

'Zoe.'

Eventually I looked up.

Josh Stanton was standing in front of me. Oh my God.

I froze, unable to speak.

After three years of watching him from a distance, his silvery-blue eyes were staring directly into mine. What was he doing out here?

He glanced quickly over his shoulder, then said, 'I just wanted to say how brilliant your set was.'

I looked round to make sure there wasn't another Zoe in the vicinity to whom he was addressing these comments, but decided he was definitely talking to me.

'The thing is,' he continued, 'I'm really into music, not seriously or anything, like you, but I do mix CDs for friends' parties – that sort of thing.'

He looked a bit shy when he spoke, maybe even nervous. I carried on staring at him, making sure my mouth was closed – that way I wouldn't blurt out anything I regretted.

He wasn't finished. 'I'm always looking for new stuff and some of the tunes you played were brilliant. It would be good to find out what they are.'

The boy I viewed with the kind of intense adoration usually reserved for pop stars and royalty was asking for *my* advice. After years of trying to get near him and worrying constantly that we inhabited separate planets, suddenly *he* looked like the one in the shadows, whilst I bathed in the limelight.

What on earth was going on? First, I pull off a great set. Next, I catch my sibling kissing my best friend. Then, Josh Stanton appears from nowhere declaring himself my number one fan. How much weirder could the evening get?

'What do you reckon?' he asked.

You have to say something, I urged myself, otherwise you'll blow this unique opportunity.

'How long have you been doing the mix CDs?' I asked.

Well done! That's probably the first sensible thing you've ever said to him.

'A couple of years,' he replied. 'They're not very good.'

I smiled back at him. 'I'm sure they're not as bad as you think.'

This was beyond incredible. Zoe Wynch was conducting a normal conversation with Josh Stanton.

'Gotta go in a minute,' he said, 'but I would love to sit down with you sometime, to talk about music.'

'It would be a pleasure,' I said, trying to maintain my composure and not appear too over-enthusiastic.

Josh Stanton wants to SIT DOWN WITH ME!

'Great,' he said with a smile, then turned and walked back inside the building.

After watching him disappear, I leaned further back against the wall and closed my eyes. Something suddenly occurred to me. Maybe my life was a bit like Dad's favourite trio. Perhaps the great loves of my life came packaged in threes. My love of music was energising and inspirational. My love of Keesha and Becky was solid and supportive (stupid arguments aside). And my love for the seemingly unattainable Josh Stanton was full of longing and suddenly much more exciting since I'd talked to him.

I stood there in the dim light, going over and over the events of the last few hours and heard a voice in the distance calling my name.

Tania Trent was beckoning to me.

She needed me on the sofa immediately. The show was about to go live and she was waving hysterically as the camera crew and sound people looked on with urgency. The floor manager was gesticulating wildly to signal my walk-on.

But I ignored them all.

At that moment all I wanted to do was experience my real world.

This was my night and I was going to enjoy it.

Acknowledgements

I'd like to thank the following people:

DJ Sarah Love who was so incredibly helpful and informative about all matters related to DJing and the DJ world. Brenda Gardner & Yasemin Uçar for seeing the big picture and taking on the project. Emma O'Bryen, for her publicity thoughts and actions. Janice Swanson, agent supreme, and Jonny Geller, the man who opened the door. Alison Goodman, Anne Joseph and Fiona Starr for endless proofing and recommendations. Tim Lawrence and Nick Lansman for listening and friendship. Big Dave C for his interest and positivity. Rachel Bowley for her fascinating take on Zoe's world, and Julia Bowley for acting as go-between. James Libson, for all matters legal. The incredible book queen, Dawn Goboume, at Alexandra Park Library, and Eleni Markou and Renata Pilay at Muswell Hill Library for massive help with research. Adam Lawrence, for the photos. Ivor Baddiel for never failing to make me laugh. And most of all Fi, for her unswerving encouragement and support both during the writing of this book and way, way beyond.

If you would like more information about books
available from Piccadilly Press and how to order
them, please contact us at:

Piccadilly Press Ltd.
5 Castle Road
London
NW1 8PR

Tel: 020 7267 4492
Fax: 020 7267 4493

Feel free to visit our website at
www.piccadillypress.co.uk